The Aldwark Tales

RICHARD TYNDALL

FIRST EDITION

GREEN CAT BOOKS

www.green-cat.co/books

CONTENTS

For
Liz, Alex and Pip.
"As long as stars are above you"

ACKNOWLEDGMENTS

After so many years in the literary wilderness there are two people who deserve my utmost gratitude. The first is my wife Liz for all her never-ending help and support and the second is my publisher and editor Lisa Greener who had the faith in me to bring this collection of stories into the world. Both have shown far more patience than any reasonable man could expect.

.

The Curious Obsession of Matthew Deacon

This was the first supernatural short story I ever wrote and, though I would probably consider myself a sceptic when it comes to ghosts, is the only one based upon anything approaching a real-life encounter.

Like all my tales, it is rooted in a real place and all the characters are based upon people I know – friends, enemies or fleeting acquaintances. The style is gentle, perhaps out of tune with modern horror which sometimes seems less about suspense and more about body count. As such it harks back to what I consider to be the golden age of supernatural writing that began with Dickens and lasted through to the era of the much underrated pulp novel. It is a style more concerned with atmosphere than atrocity, one in which there are fates both better and worse than death and where the horror, if and when it occurs, is as much psychological as serial.

Though the museum concerned is now reborn in a new guise, the staircase mentioned in the story is now lost forever, a victim of redevelopment.

The Curious Obsession of Matthew Deacon

Aldwark is a typical eastern shire town sitting serenely in the midst of manicured agricultural landscapes on the gravel terraces of the River Trespass. It has all the facilities and attractions one might expect of such a burgh. The cobbled market place – markets held Mondays, Wednesdays and Saturdays – is expansive and bounded on its western flanks by a fine, colonnaded Georgian Town Hall flying the cross of St George. The parish church, notable for the height of its steeple and also sporting the country's flag, lies just off the square behind a row of equally fine Georgian terraces. The castle, where at least one English King breathed his last, has latterly been reduced from its former glory by the misnamed Lord Protector, flushed with the success of the Puritan rebellion; its ornate carved limestone features stripped away and its stone reused in manor houses and cottages across half of the shire. Recently restored, at least to the extent of making it safe for inquisitive children and visiting tourists, it still presents a majestic façade to the river and contains within its grounds the Victorian library named for one of the town's philanthropic benefactors.

The area betrays its Danelaw origins both in its plan and in the street names – the Germanic 'gate' suffix being common throughout the town. A liberal scattering of Norse and Saxon place-names in the surrounding villages only serve to reinforce the area's Scandinavian heritage. Close by the town are Bronze Age barrows,

Roman settlements and Saxon cemeteries whilst half a dozen of the local roads began as prehistoric trackways, later Roman highways and finally Restoration turnpikes. The district has produced one Prime Minister and numerous generals, writers, artists, scientific theorists and other gentlemen of note.

It is unsurprising therefore that, in a town so immersed in history and moment, there should be a museum to collect and display the many artefacts and archaeological curiosities uncovered by more than a century of research and excavation. The institution in question is housed in a series of old school buildings – Tudor in origin - on Orchard Gate; a tree lined avenue which runs from the market place, past the back of the church and down a shallow hill towards the railway station on the northern fringes of the town. At some point in the last century or two, an architectural vandal realized that there was just enough room between the edge of the road and the old school to place a four-storey block of dark brick and misery in front of the Tudor halls and, when the complex became the home for the town's museum, it was this uninspiring building that was chosen to house the offices, archives and laboratories that would sort and store the minutiae of Aldwark's past.

When first we met, Matthew Deacon was a tall, stringy, fifteen year old whose home was in the village of Byfordham, just over the borders of the shire. He had a fascination with all things ancient and had, early in his teens, taken to hanging around the museum chatting with the curators and undertaking odd jobs for Gordon Sullivan, the town's archaeological conservator. Sullivan was an old, heavily bearded archaeologist who, in spite of being in his late middle age and facing the prospect of retirement in perhaps only a few years, was nevertheless able to instil in our young friend an abiding love of the mystery and glamour of past lives and the artefacts that were their lasting representation in our modern age. So powerful was Sullivan's influence that, when the time came for him to consider a university education which would decide the future path of his life, Deacon had no hesitation in choosing Cambridge and the formal study of the art and science of archaeology.

Looking back now it might seem that the timing of events was all too perfect to be simple coincidence, but such hindsight provides a dangerous and misleading view of the way the world works, and it should be sufficient to record the events as they occurred without further comment. So it came to pass that, just as Deacon completed his university education with well-deserved accolades, Sullivan, having hung on in his position far longer than anyone had expected, should finally reach an age at which it was considered he could no longer carry out his duties to the satisfaction of the local corporation and should take his leave of the museum. Foreswearing the many offers of further research and highly sought-after positions of employment, Matthew Deacon returned to Aldwark and, with the minimum of fuss, took up the position previously held by his friend and mentor.

One spring afternoon, half a year after he had taken up his new position, I called upon the town archaeologist at his offices and invited him to step out for afternoon tea at a small café opposite the museum. This had become something of a ritual indulgence undertaken at least once every week and was always a most pleasant experience for both of us. Deacon was unfailingly bright and cheerful, never seeming to let any adversity destroy his positive outlook on life and his company and conversation were always a pleasure. But on this occasion I was immediately struck by the aura of pent up excitement that surrounded him as he bounced down the stairs ahead of me and rushed across the road into the café. Never had I seen him more buoyant; a state of mind I mistakenly attributed to his recent notable successes on a Roman excavation on the fringes of the town. This, combined with his employment in a place where, under other circumstances, I am sure he would have paid good money to work, seemed good enough reason for him to be pleased with his lot.

But given that he surely had much news of interest to impart concerning his ongoing research and forthcoming excavations, I was momentarily surprised by his opening remarks.

Once we had settled to our table and taken delivery of our refreshments, he began.

"I saw her, Dr Trenton. As plainly as I see you sitting there in front of me with that teacake in your hand, I saw her on the stairs." He was almost breathless in his excitement.

I knew immediately to whom he was referring and smiled indulgently at my young friend's child-like enthusiasm for his recent experience. It was clear that he had just had his first encounter with Maud.

Ever since Matthew started working at the museum as a curious teenager, he had heard the stories about the girl on the stairs. Almost everyone who worked in the building had seen her at one time or another and she had become such a familiar sight for many there that she was now considered part of the fixtures and fittings; a good subject for pranks, late night stories and general discussion. No one felt any fear concerning her presence although some of the secretaries had, on occasion, expressed their dislike of staying in the offices alone.

The offices and stores occupied only one end of the four-storey building and were reached by a doorway adjacent to the main entrance to the museum. Each floor was connected by a set of spiral stairs which rose through the end of the building with small landings on each level to give access to the rooms. On the ground floor were storerooms for artefacts; row upon row of shelves and racks containing boxes of finds, donations and collections, many of which were poorly recorded and long forgotten. From the narrow, stone flagged hallway the metal stairs ascended to the first floor where the conservation laboratory and archaeology office were all contained within a single, large, concrete floored room with high ceilings and wide sash windows. Above, on the second floor, were the secretary's office and the museum records and accounts, while the third and final floor and attics contained the archives, the manuscript collections and the small private museum library.

The ghost, known affectionately as Maud – a name ascribed to the apparition so long ago that no one at the museum now knew its origins – would enter through the door on the ground floor. She would then ascend the stairs, past the laboratory on the first and the offices on the second floors, apparently en route for the archives at the top of the building. From here there was no exit other than an emergency door and fire escape which were alarmed to prevent misuse or burglary. Needless to say, Maud never reached the top floor and anyone embarking upon pursuit would find the archives empty and the emergency exit undisturbed.

At this point in our tale a description of the apparition is also probably in order, if only to help in understanding my young friend's fascination with her. What is perhaps most surprising about the reports of her appearance is that she seemed so completely normal. A young woman of an age at which thoughts turn inevitably to marriage, dressed in a knee length dress of some indefinable flower pattern – the sort of garment suitable for attracting the admiring gazes of young men on warm summer afternoons. Auburn hair fell unfettered to bare shoulders and her feet were clad in simple sandals. But in spite of these otherwise clear and consistent descriptions, no one could provide any detail of her face. No matter where one stood when encountering the vision, her head was always turned away from the observer or oriented so that her hair fell across her face, hiding her features from all possible study.

For Deacon, the spirit on the stairs had long ago developed into something of a cause for annoyance. He had nothing particularly against the ghost, quite the reverse. It was just that, in the six years since he had first entered the museum and in spite of the many hours spent working with Sullivan in the laboratory, Matthew had never seen so much as a glimpse of the famous apparition. At one point he had come to the conclusion that he was the victim of a huge and long running joke in which everyone, even his closest friends, was involved. It is to his credit that, in spite of flirting occasionally with this opinion, he never allowed it to colour his underlying attitude towards his friends. Though his patience was stretched when even the newest arrivals on the museum staff might encounter the vision after only a few days in the building. Eventually even Deacon himself became part of the tale, as the one and only person in the building who had never seen the ghost.

This state of affairs had continued after Deacon's return to Aldwark and his new, official position on the museum staff. The only difference now was that he seemed unconcerned by the continuing reports of sightings, considering them a part of background noise at the museum which barely impinged on his consciousness.

All that changed on that warm spring afternoon, six months after his arrival.

My amused expression as I regarded him across the checked cloth, tea and cakes did little to distract my friend from his excited chatter.

"I honestly thought you were all having me on you know, all those years of stories and apparent sightings and I never saw a single thing. I just thought that it had started as a joke and then no one had the courage to admit it was all a creation…" he shook his head with a wry smile as he took a long draft of hot tea.

"… until today." He stared into his cup for a moment. "I was sat at my desk, not doing anything really, just staring out of the window towards the old house in the park behind the museum, you know, the Fawcett town house. Looking at the daffodils and generally feeling very pleased about the way things had turned out. You know, with the job and coming back to Aldwark. It is everything I ever wanted, everything I dreamed about from the first time I stepped into that museum. And now it is all mine."

He looked up a little self-consciously. "Sorry, that sounds a little smug and I'm rambling as well. Anyway, I was sat there looking out across the park and I heard the door open at the bottom of the stairs. I thought perhaps you had arrived a little early and so I rose and went to the door to greet you."

He was looking into the distance over my shoulder as he recounted the encounter. "I was stood just inside the door and was about to move onto the landing. but was momentarily distracted by a tray of finds that had been delivered by the curator earlier this morning. Most of it was the normal rubbish that people bring in from their walks, but on top was a large sherd of Samian and I was about to pick it up and show it to you when she walked right past the door. She was so close that if I had had my wits about me I could have reached out and touched her."

He shook his head in a slightly dazed fashion, as if the memory of the apparition had physically stunned him. "I don't quite know what happened to me. It was so unexpected. I didn't move, didn't say a word. I just watched as she drifted past and continued up the stairs to the next floor."

"Drifted?" I remarked on his choice of words. "Was she floating then, could you see her feet?"

"Oh no, no, that's not what I meant. I'm sorry, that was a poor choice of words given the circumstances. No, she was walking just like you and I except... except of course neither you nor I could ever walk in such a graceful manner. Such modes of locomotion are reserved only for the fairer sex. She glided across the floor like an angel or... well yes, a ghost I suppose, but that wasn't it. It was just that she trod that landing so gracefully, the way that only a girl of perfect bearing could tread. With only the softest pad of her step as if she were barefoot.

Such grace, such poise. Truly she is not a ghost but an angel."

Deacon's rapt expression showed he had been touched far more than I would have expected by the vision on the stairs. He had always struck me as a somewhat overly romantic fellow, but this reaction seemed far more extreme than I would have expected. I felt a momentary twinge of concern for the archaeologist but dismissed it almost immediately as I considered that, in all the years that Maud had been haunting the museum, not once had any harm befallen anyone who had encountered her.

"Did you see her face?" I enquired.

"No, no, she had her head turned away from me all the time and by the time I got my wits back she had already climbed to the second floor. I went after her, right to the very top of the building but... well, you know the story as well as I. There was no sign of her. She climbed the stairs and disappeared."

I smiled warmly at him. "Of course you realise this is the end of an era don't you?"

"What do you mean?"

"You were almost famous at the museum. Didn't you know? They were still talking about you even before you came back to work here; the only person never to have seen the girl on the stairs. Now that you have finally seen her we will have to consign that particular tale to the archives."

Deacon smiled briefly at the thought but then returned immediately to his subject. "Who is she, Doctor?" he asked earnestly. "What happened to her and why is she condemned to climb those stairs for all eternity?"

"Well, I'm not sure about all eternity, Matthew," I laughed indulgently, "after all she has only been seen for the last century or so."

He ignored my attempts at a joke. "But someone must know something about her. She has been seen by almost everyone at the museum, surely someone must have done some research to find out who she was?"

I shook my head and finished the last of my tea. "Not that I am aware of. I know old Sullivan did a cursory examination of the archives many years ago when he first came to the museum, but I gather that when he found nothing he returned to more interesting subjects and decided it was just one of those mysteries that was destined never to be solved."

My companion looked shocked at this, almost scornful. "How can anyone think that this isn't interesting? This is fascinating, it is a genuine mystery and I am sure there must be some explanation. If she is a ghost, then she has to have been a living person once. There must be records somewhere of what happened to her. All I need to do is look hard enough. I will find out who she was. I must."

I had thought to try to dissuade the young man from becoming too immersed in this mystery. No good could come of such an obsessive quest and I did not doubt that it was in the nature of the archaeologist with his notions of romantic honour to pursue this search to the detriment of all other tasks.

I should have said something then, I see that now. It is an omission that will haunt me every single day for the rest of my life. But for some reason at that moment I chose to keep my own council. Perhaps it was his forthright determination, perhaps, conversely, the thought that it was something that would pass after a few days of failure. And if he did succeed, well, I would be just as interested as the next man in finally hearing the true story of the girl on the stairs.

And so I said nothing more on the subject. We discussed a few other topics of mutual interest involving the museum and acquaintances around the town, but it was clear that the act of revealing his encounter with the ghost and the subsequent statements of intent had served to crystallise Matthew Deacon's determination, to focus his mind upon the task at hand and so, in short order, we parted with declarations of mutual friendship and promises to meet again the following week for further discussion over tea and cakes.

2

We did indeed meet the following week, although my friend seemed distracted during our afternoon tea and it was clear that he could raise little enthusiasm for our normal discourse. Mindful of his intense interest in the supernatural inhabitant of the stairwell, I had thought that perhaps this would be the sole topic of conversation but for the first twenty minutes or so he made no mention of his researches and much of the time seemed more interested in the contents of his teacup than in his companion sat across the small table.

Eventually I decided that the only way to salvage something of the afternoon was to raise the subject myself. I hoped this might provoke a more forthright response but, even on this most topical of subjects his responses were at best half-hearted and it was left to me to carry the conversation as best I could while he limited himself to single word replies and long, thoughtful silences. Under the circumstances it was almost a relief when he declared, upon the hour, that he must return to his office and continue his work.

Over the next month or so our contact was slight. Deacon seemed completely engrossed in his research, the subject of which was by now clear to everyone in the museum. I decided against inviting him out for tea again and instead limited myself to visits to his laboratory where I could attempt to engage in conversation whilst he continued his enquiries amongst the books and papers he had secured from the archives and the local library. My initial concern that he might be neglecting his other work and so put his position at risk with regard to the directors of the museum and the town corporation, proved ill-founded as it seemed he was quite capable of undertaking both his paid employ and his own private researches at the same time to the detriment of neither. But it was also clear from his comments and general demeanour, his short-tempered replies and spontaneous declarations of disgust that he was having no success in his quest to identify the mysterious girl.

Try as he might, Deacon could find no record of events or persons that might account for the apparition. No stories of Georgian feuds ending, as they invariably did, in the murder of those most innocent. No tales of unrequited Victorian love whose final act was the tragic demise by terminal self-harm of the rejected maiden, cast aside and ruined by a callous 'gentleman'. No Edwardian crimes of passion whose epilogue was a short walk to the gallows on a frosty autumn morn for a man who had already consigned his wife to her eternal rest. Not even a wartime melodrama, played out against a backdrop of blackout curtains and rousing Churchillian speeches, making liberal use of arsenic or cyanide to bring matters to an abrupt and fatal conclusion. No crimes, no accidents, no history of any kind. For all his many hours of research in the box files and journals, the books and diaries that filled the dimly lit attic spaces of the museum, Deacon could find nothing that could help in his quest to identify the ghostly girl who had started to form the focus of a dangerous obsession.

Just how dangerous we would not realise until it was far, far too late.

Had Deacon's obsession limited itself to his vain attempts to uncover the corporeal origins of the ghostly girl then it is possible that things may have resolved themselves in something less than tragedy. It was certainly the case that the longer he delved into the archives the more he neglected his other researches and the work for which he was handsomely paid. It is also inevitable that, had things continued along this path then, matters may well have reached the point where his employers took an unhealthy interest in his activities. But for now, perhaps unfortunately given the eventual outcome, the rest of the staff endeavoured to ensure that any lapses or mistakes on the part of their archaeologist were dealt with promptly before they gave rise to comment or complaint.

But it was not in Matthew Deacon's nature to hammer away at a problem forever without resolution. Equally it was most certainly not in his nature to abandon a task when he was so sure that it could be resolved to his satisfaction, if only he could approach it in the right manner. And this was a task to which he had set his whole heart and soul over these last few months. Though I did not know it at the time, he therefore concluded that his continuing investigations amongst the parchments and papers of half a dozen institutions in the town would bring no satisfactory conclusion to his enquiries and so, after one last fruitless examination of the church records, he decided to embark upon another, more direct course of action.

We had last met at the museum in mid-July when he had railed at great length against the poor state of the archives and the thoughtlessness of long dead diarists who had seen fit to ignore the tragic death of a girl so young and innocent. Where exactly he got these ideas from is not clear to me and seemed to be more the results of a fevered brain than any annotated research. As a result, before the afternoon had drawn to a close, I found myself arguing more forcefully than ever before that the archaeologist should take a step back from his obsessive enquiries and adopt a more measured attitude to what was, after all, a perfectly harmless phenomenon that had been in existence since long before either of us had first entered the museum, and which was almost inevitably bound to continue long after we had left this life. Hoping to lighten the atmosphere, I might even have attempted a joke along the lines that we would surely find the answer to all these questions when we had joined the young lady in the afterlife but that I was content that such a resolution would be many, many years hence.

My comments, it seems, were ill-judged and only served to inflame my friend's passions on the subject.

Consequently, whilst no physical assault was made, I was forced to withdraw from the laboratory without further reconciliation in the face of a most forthright and brutal verbal assault on my character. I will admit that as a result I decided to wash my hands of the matter for some days but, as is my nature in these advancing years, I quickly forgot the slight hurt that had been caused by Deacon's rash accusations and resolved that the best way to bring matters to a respectable and satisfactory conclusion was to attempt to aid him in his researches to the best of my ability. At least in such circumstances I would be able to maintain some slight control over matters and reassure myself that young Matthew was not further endangering his position at the museum or his physical wellbeing.

Little did I know that he had already embarked upon his foolhardy plan and that it was already far too late for me to restore him to his former state of mental stability. In any event, I only had a single, all too brief meeting with my increasingly distant young friend after he made his fateful decision.

I had not seen him for perhaps six weeks and, as a result of consulting with his colleagues at the museum and those few, close relatives with whom he would occasionally correspond, I was becoming increasingly concerned at the state of both his physical and mental health. Each time I had attempted to see him at his laboratory I was informed that he was either absent or unavailable to receive visitors. Phone calls were redirected to the museum switchboard and, although the operator was almost painfully keen to help, Deacon adamantly refused to take calls and all messages requesting he contact me went unanswered. After a fortnight or so I resorted to writing to my friend, setting out my concerns as clearly and a forcefully as I could and pleading for an audience at the earliest possible opportunity.

Still there was no response.

Although I could not give up entirely on my friend, I had reached the conclusion that, short of physically forcing my way into his presence - an option that, given my advancing years, was impractical as well as unsavoury – I had no choice but to accept that, for now at least, I could do no more to help him. Although I sat on the museum board of friends and maintained an active participation in the Aldwark Archaeology and Local History Society, I held no official position with regard to the museum and could only enter the private offices upon specific invitation.

The solution to my problem, at least of a sort, came in the form of an approach from the directors of the museum. A letter arrived at my town house one Saturday afternoon asking that, if I could spare the time, I should attend a meeting at the museum that evening to discuss a matter of some delicacy. No further information was given in the missive, but it was signed on behalf of the three directors and it was with they that I was to have the meeting. Under the circumstances it seemed clear that there was only one likely topic of conversation.

On a warm summer evening in the dying days of August, with the air sweet with the scent of honeysuckle along Church Walk, I approached the museum with a combination of relief and trepidation. It was a matter of great satisfaction to me that I should at last have some means of approaching Deacon and ascertaining his state of mind. At the same time, I was concerned that matters should have come to such a juncture that the directors of the museum had become involved, a situation that could only prove harmful to the archaeologist's long-term employment prospects.

In the event the meeting, though brief, was relaxed and friendly. All three directors were old acquaintances, and all knew of my affection for the young archaeologist. It was for this reason that they had called upon me for assistance. Though they chose not to reveal any great detail, they admitted that the museum had suffered greatly over recent weeks as Deacon had withdrawn to his laboratory. The consequence of this being that he had failed to carry out any of the regular tasks assigned to his position. They realised that the other members of staff had been attempting to conceal the problems and considered that this was admirable, if misplaced loyalty for which there would be no recriminations. But once they had gained some notion of the nature of the affliction that had so altered the behaviour of their promising young employee they had decided that, in the manner of such establishments, 'something must be done'.

It appeared that that 'something' was my good self.

They had called me to the museum that late summer evening in the hope that I would go straight away to the laboratory and speak with Matthew Deacon; explain the gravity of the situation to him, seek to gain some idea of his state of mind, perhaps persuade him to take a few weeks leave of absence from the museum, on full pay of course. In short, they sought my good advice in the hope that this might convince the obsessive archaeologist that things could not go on as they were. Something – as the phrase was once again repeated to me – must be done.

I realised, of course, that these gentlemen must be unaware of the breech in friendship that had occurred between Deacon and myself at our last meeting, but I also knew that this was not the time to raise the point. I had been offered the opportunity I had been seeking for many weeks and would not now set it aside for the sake of an unspoken white lie. I agreed without hesitation to their proposal and left the directors' private offices in the museum en route for the laboratory and a commission to save the career and, quite possibly, the sanity of my young friend.

3

Entering the stairwell and ascending to the first floor, I was quite unprepared for the scene that greeted me as I stood at the door to the laboratory. What had previously been a well ordered and organised place of research and restoration was now little more than a midden. The structure of the room has been rearranged in such a radical and unconventional manner as to make it almost impossible for its occupant to carry out any of his prescribed tasks. The huge wooden bench, which had dominated the centre of the room for longer than I could remember and which had held all the equipment, glassware and chemical tanks necessary for the conservation of the most fragile artefacts, was now resting crookedly against the far wall under the tall shutterless windows. Though it was now mid evening and the sun had passed from the sky, it was clear that its shrivelling heat had already done irreparable damage to a delicate fragment of medieval tapestry that Deacon had been charged with preserving, and even from the door I could almost see the colours fading from the cloth as it lay unnoticed and forgotten on the worktop.

Boxes of finds, the treasured results of half a dozen excavations which, until just a few weeks before, had been carefully stacked and catalogued on shelves along one wall of the laboratory awaiting closer examination and description, were now piled in a confused and unrecorded mound in in one corner of the room. Already some of the boxes had split and sherds of Roman Mortaria and scarlet Samian ware – perhaps even the piece that had distracted Deacon on the day he first saw the spirit – lay scattered across the floor. Carefully ordered volumes of books and journals were now piled around the room, seemingly dumped anywhere when no place could immediately be found for them in Deacon's new 'order'. In short, the whole scene was one of the utmost turmoil.

But whatever the confusion into which the laboratory had descended it was immediately clear exactly what had been the aim of this reorganisation, though that term can be applied only loosely. For Deacon's desk, the dark chunk of Victorian furniture at which he would sit to write reports, collate data and answer his correspondence, had been dragged forth from its position under the windows. It was a position it had occupied, as best I could tell, for many decades and to which it was admirably suited given the natural light that would illuminate whatever work was being conducted there. Now it had been dragged, pushed and cajoled across the concrete floor, through scattered and crushed artefacts and torn papers, to be installed in a new position, just inside the room right in front of the door leading onto the landing and stairwell. It was a position from which the occupant of the chair, which stood behind the desk, could observe the stairs at all times and gain access to them in a moment.

It took no great feat of deduction to realise why Deacon had so disrupted his working environment, though the realisation of what he had been attempting since last we met sent an icy hand stroking down my spine. Unable to uncover the secrets of the apparition that continued to haunt both the stairwell and his own tortured psyche, the archaeologist had decided on a more direct approach to the problem. His aim was simple; to intercept the ghost of the girl on the stairs and try to communicate with her directly. To a sane man it would seem a dangerous and foolhardy course but to Deacon, now sunk into an obsessive madness from which he could find no release, it was a simple plan that would provide the answer to all his questions and so release him from his burden.

The man himself was there in the room, slumped across his desk just in front of me, clearly alive – I had entertained momentary fears about that point as I climbed the stairs - but also in a deep, sonorous sleep. I stood for a moment looking at him, trying to form some plan as to how to approach him without causing alarm, but even as I watched he stirred, muttered something unintelligible and raised his head to regard me through half opened, black rimmed eyes.

"Wh...who's there...who, oh..." he sat upright in the chair, rubbed his hand across his face and focused his eyes upon me more steadily. "Doctor? Doctor Trenton? What are you doing here? I thought... I thought it was her...I..." The sentence remained unfinished and a pregnant pause hovered between us.

"Good evening Matthew." I regarded him for a moment with a mixture of disappointment and concern. "I would ask how you are but I can see from the state of your office and your person that all is not well with you."

He mumbled something again and rose. He did at least have the good grace to look embarrassed. Stepping further into the room in response to an assumed invitation, I noticed that a low cot was arranged along the wall behind the desk. I concluded that it was many nights since the archaeologist had occupied his lodgings above the chemist's shop in the corner of the market square.

He was moving into the centre of the laboratory; the only relatively clear space amongst the jetsum of his ruined work. I winced as a grinding snap marked the destruction of another piece of pottery under his uncaring boots. I had planned to approach things carefully so as to avoid any chance of the meeting degenerating once again into a confrontation, but now that I saw the depths into which my friend's life had descended, I forgot my caution and launched a desperate plea for sanity.

"What has happened to you Matthew? What have you done to your laboratory, to your work? Can't you see that you have put everything at risk with this mad obsession of yours?"
He stood amidst the wreckage of his life, eyes closed, unshaven face turned to the heavens, bearing a look of desperate resignation. When he spoke his voice was broken, reflecting his shattered spirit.

"She would not let me be. Never, not for a moment. She was always there, waiting, watching, whispering to me. Urging me on to… to find the answers. To help her. Doctor," he looked at me directly for the first time, "I was only trying to help her, only trying to do something right, something honourable. Would you have acted in any other way if you had been the one she asked?"

I regarded him with pity for a moment, convinced that his mind had finally broken under the strain of these last, lost weeks of solitude. At what point he had begun to create the voice that he claimed had guided him in his search I could not tell. Certainly, I believe it was at some time after our last meeting. But that was immaterial. It was clear now that, as he had become more desperate, he had searched within himself for reassurance and had found a cause, a mission if you like, to free the spirit from its eternal climb into oblivion. And when he had finally realised that his searching would yield no salvation for either the spirit or himself he had chosen this new course.

When I did not immediately answer his question, he continued. "I see her so often now, every day, sometimes many times a day." He laughed, a bitter cackle devoid of joy. "Ironic isn't it? For all those years, the only person in the history of this whole benighted place who has never seen her and now? Now I can't stop seeing her. Day and night, over and over again she opens that front door and climbs those stairs right past that door," he pointed a shaking hand towards the entrance behind me, "half a dozen times a day sometimes and just as many at night. And every time I hear her coming I try to get onto the landing to catch her... I try to get out of the door so I am close enough to see her face, anything that might give me a clue as to who she is. But she is always past me before I can reach her. No matter how hard I tried, how quick I was to realise that she was coming through the door, I could never get onto the landing before she was climbing the second flight of stairs. And when I tried to follow her up it was as if I were walking through tar, as if it were a dream, one of those dreams from which you think you will never awaken." He slumped back against the wooden bench and gave a low moan of despair, "perhaps it is a dream. Perhaps I am fated never to awaken."

"It is no dream Matthew. This is your life and you need to reclaim it. If you do not then… well, I was going to say that your future employment at the museum was in jeopardy, but I fear that may be the very least of our concerns."

Deacon remained silent. The news that he might forfeit his position at the museum did not seem to give rise to any greater concern than that which he already felt and I suspect that, at this moment, he would consider it a blessing if he escaped having lost nothing more than his reputation and his position.

"In truth, it may already be too late to save your position here at the museum and I feel that, even were you able to retain your post, it might be unwise for you to remain. This place, these offices, I fear you would soon succumb once again to the madness that has led you to this sorry state. It might be for the best if you were to seek employment elsewhere away from that accursed staircase and its spirit."

The gaze he bestowed upon me was filled with sad resignation. "You are right of course. I cannot remain here after all that has occurred."

Drawing himself up from the bench, he had apparently decided upon his course of action, though it was clear that it was not one which he would have followed willingly. Nevertheless, I was relieved to see this new determination in my young friend which spoke much to me of his resilience under the most difficult of circumstances.

He turned to look about his laboratory, taking in, perhaps for the first time in many weeks, the chaos that his madness had wrought upon the place. He shook his head slightly and turned to me with a new air of resolve.

"Thank you, doctor, thank you for coming to help me. You may return to the directors and inform them that I will put my affairs in order here and will then meet with them in the morning to discuss the swift resolution of this matter. You may assure them that no scandal will be associated with the museum and that I will follow their direction, and yours, in the matter of my future."

I regarded the young man for a moment, searching for any sign of deception but saw nothing in his tired but honest features that would indicate any falsehood.

"Good. I am greatly relieved that you have come to your senses over this matter and I am sure that you are making the right decision. You will find that once you leave this place behind you the memory will quickly fade." I smiled warmly at him. "You are a young man with a great future ahead of you. This small lapse of good sense will soon seem nothing more than a bad dream, I assure you."

I turned towards the door and, when I reached the landing, looked back at Deacon who had moved to behind his strangely placed desk. "I will of course speak on your behalf with the directors and I am sure that they will do all they can to ensure your reputation is untarnished and that a new place of employment is found for you with all possible speed. Do what you must to put the laboratory in some semblance of order, but then do go back to your rooms. Do not stay here tonight.

There is nothing for you here now. The nightmare is over. Tomorrow you start your life anew."

For the first time since I had disturbed him, a genuine smile appeared on Deacon's face. It was slight but it was there, more in his eyes than on his lips but a good sign none the less.

"Goodnight Dr Trenton, and thank you."

"Goodnight Matthew. Sleep well. I look forward to taking tea with you tomorrow."

"Perhaps. We can discuss that tomorrow." He turned away from the landing, back into the room, not bothering to see me descend into the shadows of the stairs and leave the building by that strange, haunted door.

4

That was the last time I ever saw Matthew Deacon in life or in death. The following morning his laboratory was found to be returned to its former, well ordered state and there was little sign of the turmoil that had been so apparent only the evening before. All the artefacts were returned to their racks, the books to their shelves and the equipment and furniture to the positions it had occupied for so many years before Deacon's mania. Anyone entering the office on that warm August morning would have had no suggestion that anything had been amiss. But there was one thing that was missing from this scene of scientific study. Of the archaeologist himself there was no sign.

Initially this did not give cause for concern, as I had already reported to the directors on the previous evening that I had advised him to return to his lodgings for some sleep once he had finished in the laboratory. When I arrived at the museum at just before ten he had still not made an appearance, but given his obvious exhaustion this was not unexpected, if a little foolish given the precariousness of his position with his superiors. By eleven I had begun to have some concerns and asked that one of the curators be dispatched to his lodgings to enquire as to his health. The man returned inside twenty minutes to report that Mr Deacon had not returned to his lodgings on the previous evening, in fact had not been seen by his landlord or neighbours for a number of weeks.

On hearing this news and with a cold fear rising within me, I accompanied the directors up to the laboratory to examine the scene in the hope of ascertaining some clue as to Deacon's whereabouts. It did not take a great detective to find the evidence for which we were searching. Lying upon the polished top of his large Victorian desk, now returned to its rightful position in front of the tall sash windows, was an envelope, addressed to myself and within it a single sheet of paper bearing a handwritten note. In a moment of bemused detachment, I noted the fine steady hand in which the letter had been written. There was no sign of mania or undue mental stress and it could so easily have been a note inviting me to tea at the café that afternoon. To my eternal regret it was no such thing.

Dear Dr Trenton,

I have chosen to address this last missive to your good self as, above all men, you have shown me such kindness and tolerance in these difficult times. For that I will be forever grateful.

I know this will be hard for you to understand but your visit last night really did achieve exactly the effect you desired. It freed me from my demons and allowed me to see clearly for the first time what I must do to ensure an end to this troubling state of affairs.

It is also clear that your visit had an effect on more than just myself. After you left I began to arrange my affairs in just the manner we discussed and, as I am sure you will agree, I have returned the laboratory to a state in which my successor should have no difficulty in picking up the tasks that I have unfortunately had to leave to his good care.

Although I was already aware of what the night would bring, I was reassured when, shortly after ten, I heard the familiar sound of the door at the foot of the stairs being opened and that light footfall upon the steps leading to my landing. I approached the door and found, just as I had expected that, for the first time, the lady in question had not passed me by on her ascent into the darkness but was instead stood at the foot of the second flight of stairs waiting for me. She was waiting for me, Robert. And as I approached the door she turned her face to mine and I looked at last into those wonderful deep pools of light and love that were her eyes.

She awaits me now, just outside the door for she will not enter. I am to go with her into her world and I go, you may be assured, with a fearful yet joyful heart. At last I will know the truth of who she is and what fate brought her to this place. One day, perhaps, you too will know that answer. I will be awaiting you when you decide to take that journey.

Thank you again for all your kindness and be assured that I will remain, always, your friend,

Matthew

There was no more. No sign of my young friend was ever found, though the museum and the police conducted their enquiries with the utmost diligence. The idea that he had actually left this life in the company of a ghostly apparition was never seriously considered and the authorities had little choice but to leave matter as unsolved.

After Matthew's disappearance, the post of conservator was left vacant and the duties of the position were transferred to the Shire Archaeologist and the university authorities. The laboratory was converted into storage rooms and, because there was now no need for so many secretarial staff, the offices were also transferred to the main museum buildings. As a result, the old Victorian stairwell was visited far less often and encounters with 'Maud' became less frequent.

Not that they ended entirely. There were still sightings of the girl in the summer dress climbing the stairs into oblivion but the reports that returned to me were now subtly different. In all the many years that she had been climbing those stairs, not a word had ever been reported passing the lips of the apparition. But now, more often than not, sightings were accompanied by the sound of gentle laughter or whispered speech, as one would associate with lovers on a country walk. No word could be clearly heard but the tone was warm and carefree.

And on more than one occasion, although the spirit was apparently alone on the stairs, it was reported that her words were clearly answered by another voice, equally loving, warm and carefree. The voice of a young man. The voice, I have no doubt, of my good friend Matthew Deacon.

The Gallows Grave

As a sometime archaeologist, I have what some might consider to be an irrational hatred of those metal detectorists who spend their time searching for rare fragments of the past which they can then sell for a few pounds, thus removing from the record vital clues about our ancestors. They are a modern plague upon our history and, whilst the libertarian in me prevents advocating the outright banning of this particular pastime, that does not mean I cannot enjoy imagining the most heinous of fates for those who wander the countryside stripping it of its history for nothing more than tawdry personal profit.

In these most litigious of times, most books and films these days tend to have a foot note somewhere stating that 'Any resemblance to persons living or dead is purely coincidental'. I often feel this is one of the most blatant lies perpetrated by writers. I doubt there are many writers who do not draw on the characteristics of friends and acquaintances for inspiration and an easy way to add depth to their creations.

However, in the case of this story, I feel it necessary to state for the record that the characters described herein are nothing more than figments of my imagination. Whether you believe me or not is another matter entirely, but should anyone reading this tale feel I have drawn rather too closely upon their particular moral and social deficiencies, then rest assured that I am quite prepared to follow the lead of St Peter and deny all knowledge of you before the cock crows.

The Gallows Grave

Some two miles southwest of Aldwark, along the old straight road that splits the county in two, lies the village of Fernbank. Dating back to Saxon or perhaps even Roman times, these days the village has expanded far beyond its original boundaries to fill a broad strip of land on the ridge between the road and the river flood plain. The village has lost much of its character as a result of the expansion and is now little different to hundreds of similar settlements across the shires which have fallen victim to ever growing populations of newcomers with scant knowledge of country ways and country life.

There were other ways in which Fernbank resembled other communities across England. For there was a man – a poor description but it will have to suffice for the purposes of this narrative – a man who went by the name of Bobby Grayling. There is a Bobby Grayling in every parish in England. They may not look the same, may bear no external resemblance to each other whatsoever, but in nature, mannerisms and downright crookedness all these men – for they are invariably male – are brothers in everything but name. Normally there is never more than one of these malignant creatures in each village; no community being able to survive with more than a single such drain on its physical and mental wellbeing. In Fernbank, Bobby Grayling was the sickness that sapped the strength of the community.

Grayling did not work. At least he undertook no sort of paid employment like his neighbours. He had decided very early in life that work was - to quote him when he was being less than circumspect - 'a mug's game'. So these days Grayling was 'unfit' for work as a result of a minor accident many years earlier, which had caused such irreparable damage to his back as to make it impossible for him to hold down a job. Or that was what he claimed and, as is the manner in this day and age, his claims were certified by a doctor too busy to pay real attention and more concerned for people with real injuries and illnesses than for one man who just wanted to get one over on the system. And so his career-ending injuries were accepted without question by the authorities, certified with a note in a file and set in stone forever more. Of course, suggestions were made for light forms of work away from the factory floor, but he could easily deflect such suggestions with a few carefully placed medical conditions. Manual work was right out as his back would never take the strain. The same applied to any office work that required him to sit for any great length of time as that made his back go into spasm. Walking was agreeable but not when carrying anything. He ensured that, whilst making heartfelt declarations of his wish to earn his keep, he was seen as such a burden to any prospective employer that he was assured of never finding a real job.

In the end the authorities admitted defeat – though in truth they had never really tried very hard to avoid the decision. Bobby was signed off on permanent sick leave and received a generous payment from his former employers and a healthy pension from the state. And all before he had even completed his fourth decade of life.

After a year or so of doing nothing much and generally enjoying life, Grayling found that the money from his employer was starting to run low and the pension, generous as it was, was nowhere near enough to keep him and his family in the manner to which they would like to become accustomed. As a result, he looked around for something he could do that would provide a little bit of money on the side but would not involve anything too strenuous. By chance a cousin had recently acquired a metal detector which, considering the force at which it must have hit the ground when it fell off the back of the lorry, was in remarkably good condition. A touch of gentle persuasion, combined with the payment of a small fee, ensured that the instrument was quickly acquired by Grayling and he embarked on his new career as a treasure hunter.

Grayling now became a particularly low form of pond life in the deep, wide pool that is archaeology. He was driven by one thing and one thing alone; the prospect of finding something valuable enough that he might make a few pounds or, even better, a few thousand pounds from a sale to a private 'collector'. It was theft in everything but name and, as such, was immensely attractive.

So, over the next few years, this man whose injuries prevented him undertaking any form of manual labour was to be seen in fields all over the parish and beyond digging away in search of buried treasure. This poor invalid who could carry nothing more than a cup of tea was to be seen on a warm summer's evening striding proudly across the fields bearing a weighty pack filled to the brim with pot, stone and metal to be examined later in the safety of his home. This cripple who could not sit for more than a few minutes without his back going into painful spasm could be found, hour after hour, at his desk poring over some tiny scrap of bronze buckle or a medieval coin; cleaning and preparing to ensure he got the very best of prices from the select group of collectors who he hoped to tempt into discrete visits to his home to purchase the rare and beautiful items he had found in the fields around Aldwark.

Nor was Grayling restricted to simply combing the open fields in the hope of a chance discovery. Early in his newfound career he had realised that if he really wanted to make some money, he needed to be searching in those places known to have been of importance centuries earlier; the prehistoric burial mounds, Roman villas and forts, Saxon cemeteries and deserted medieval villages. These were the places that would yield the best rewards for the least work. These were the places that Bobby and his metal detector needed to visit. Unfortunately for Grayling, such sites are of value to more than just treasure hunters. Centuries of neglect and treasure hunting by Gentleman Antiquarians had led government to pass laws protecting these places from the worst ravages of greed and well-meant but incompetent archaeological research. Designated as historic monuments, most of the really interesting sites were now legally out of bounds to Grayling and his faithful detector.

Not, of course, that he intended to let that stop him for a minute. It just meant he had to carry out more of his detecting under the cover of darkness or poor weather. Fog was a positive blessing. It may have made his task a little less enjoyable at times but if he was lucky the rewards might compensate for any temporary discomfort. And so it was that Bobby Grayling became that most disreputable of practitioners in an already tarnished hobby: A Nighthawk.

It heartens the author to report that, in his new vocation, Bobby Grayling was a notable failure. Assisted by his cousin Ronny - a congenital idiot whose opposing thumb and upright stance mistakenly led people to assume the presence of some form of human intelligence - in a less than a year he was able to strip the parish of Fernbank of anything resembling archaeological heritage. To an archaeologist what he found was almost priceless, but to Bobby it was little better than garbage; bits of pot, bones and the occasional coin. The sort of thing that might sell for a few pounds but would never be enough to make a living out of. Still, he was nothing if not persistent. Once Fernbank had been pillaged, it was a natural step to move further afield and start the scouring of adjacent parishes up and down the old Roman road. There were sites aplenty for anyone with the right tools and sufficient lack of moral rectitude, but a trove of any real value always managed to elude the nighthawk. Crime, it seemed, just would not pay. And so, as time went by and Bobby failed to dig up his fortune, his thoughts began to turn to the one site he had always sworn he would never touch.

It was a site that had particularly fascinated and haunted Grayling for many a year, even before he had discovered his true vocation as a grave robber. As a boy he had been afraid of little in the village. He was, after all, a consummate bully and sneak, and had always maintained a coterie of associates – I hesitate to call them friends – willing to watch his back, for a suitable price of course. But there had been one thing that 'associates' could not protect him from, one fear that had been with him for as long as he could remember, and that was undiminished by time or adulthood. A place that both attracted and repelled him in equal measure and which lay close by in the adjacent parish of Stoches.

-

Upon leaving the south western fringes of Fernbank, the old straight road crosses an area of low marshy land close by the river. The location makes the river side meadows prone to regular flooding during the months of autumn and winter, and waters regularly lap against the raised bank of the road which acts in the manner of a dyke, protecting the fields and villages behind from the worst of the winter inundation. Only on the rarest of occasions in the most severe of seasons have the waters overwhelmed the road to bring misery to the hamlets beyond. On the far side of the marshes the road passes through the ancient village of Stoches, which sits upon a sandy ridge close by the site of the Roman fort of Pontus Niger. Unlike its neighbouring village, Stoches has escaped the worst of the development that has afflicted the rest of the district and, even today, remains a compact settlement with all the benefits of a shire hamlet.

This quiet village, disturbed only by the incessant growl of traffic negotiating the curves and bends that curl past the local pub, enters our story as the home of one of Grayling's uncles, now long dead but pertinent to the tale, as it was to his house that young Bobby was forced to walk every Friday evening, while his parents drank themselves into oblivion at Fernbank's riverside inn. The house and the uncle were both unremarkable. Actually that is unfair to the man, who was the one good thing in Grayling's wretched life, and who did all in his power to deflect the boy from his inevitable slide into indolence and crime. But for the sake of this tale, further description of either the uncle or his residence are unnecessary.

What is of note for our story is the field to the south of the road just as it rose up onto the bank and entered the village. For in this field was a mound, some fifty feet in diameter and perhaps ten feet in height above the rest of the pasture. Known locally as the Gallows Grave, it was this mound and the field it occupied that formed the focus for all Bobby Grayling's greatest fears and nightmares. Every Friday night he would make the mile and a half walk from Fernbank, down the footpath to meet the road at the edge of the marshes and then along the verge, across the low ground until he came in sight of the ridge and the first lights of the houses of Stoches village. In the middle of the year this could be a pleasant enough walk. In the days of his youth there were few cars on the road and none of the great lorries which now made walking the route so hazardous. On a warm summer's evening the prospect of an evening with his uncle, perhaps some fishing on the river below the old hall or a wander through the woods behind the water meadows, was enough to suck him across the marshes in a mood of excited anticipation. But as the year drew to a close and the evenings grew dark before he had even finished his lessons, he came to loathe that walk along the old Roman road. With few cars and no street lights, the trip became a stumble through the darkness struggling to avoid the potholes and pitfalls in the roadside. As often as not, winds whipped off the open fields to the north across the river, driving rain, sleet or snow with them. However much he might plead, whatever the weather and however unwell he might be, Grayling's parents always insisted that he make that walk across the marshes to his uncle's house while they adjourned to the fireside at the inn.

Truth be told, Bobby could cope with the darkness, the weather and the cold. They were annoyances to be endured but would do little lasting harm, and there was always the prospect of hot toast and Ovaltine once he reached the warmth of his uncle's house. But before he reached that haven, there was one hurdle that had to be overcome, one terror that had to be faced every Friday evening, alone and in the dark.

Bobby Grayling had to walk past the field containing the Gallows Grave.

If you had asked him why that particular feature in that particular field should evoke such terror, young Grayling could probably have cited little more than deep-seated but apparently unfounded feelings of unease and repeated the common local legends about the place. It undoubtedly possessed a dark and unsettling history, having for many years been the site of a gallows upon which highwaymen and other 'ne'er do wells' were hung after a short and usually biased trial at the local hall. In the eighteenth century the 4th Earl of Stoches, one John Lovell, had earned the appellation of 'Gibbet John' as a result of the number of men he had successfully prosecuted for robbery, assault or just plain indolence on the Aldwark turnpike. All had ended their days hanging from the beam on Gallows Grave, in the process providing the mound with both its name and its bloody reputation. Gibbet John himself had disappeared in mysterious circumstances in that very field one foggy winter's night in 1784 and no trace of his body had ever been discovered. After his death the mound had been used as the site for a post mill, taking advantage of the bitter winds that swept up onto the ridge from the marshes. But it was reputed an accursed place and after only a few years the mill was lost in a fire, the miller escaping with his life but nothing more. After that, the mound had been left well alone and even successive generations of farmers refused to plough across that part of the field, leaving it instead as a circle of pasture on which the livestock refused to feed. Grayling knew the stories well enough and also the rumours of strange noises that drifted out of the field on misty nights when, in spite of the lack of wind, a creaking could be heard coming from the direction of the mound, like a wooden beam straining under the weight of a swinging corpse.

And so, every Friday evening Bobby Grayling would approach the bottom of the rise in darkness, stealing himself for a mad rush up the hill, past the field and into the village, not stopping or looking back until he reached the safety of his uncle's door.

Grayling had never forgotten those fearful winter walks. Even now, more than thirty years later, the thought of the Gallows Grave was still enough to produce dark moods and darker dreams. For this reason, the parish of Stoches had remained mercilessly free of the ravages of metal detectors. Within the parish boundaries were many protected sites including the Roman fort, the medieval remains of what had once, before the terrible plagues of the 14th century, been a far more substantial village and even a battlefield where the King of England once put his rebellious subjects to the sword by the thousand. In spite of all of this, Grayling had steered well clear of Stoches and its blood-soaked mound.

Yet there was something about that field and the mound it contained that held an almost hypnotic sway over the nighthawk. Part of it was a need to confront his fears, a need to lay to rest the ghosts that had haunted him since childhood. But more than that, much more than that, was greed; the one underlying emotion that had driven him for so many years. The thought that the mound might contain something of great value; that it would finally provide that one priceless hoard of treasure that would see Grayling set for life. And yet his fear still held him back, still gripped his heart and persuaded him against exploration of the Gallows Grave. Then, finally, he found the one piece of information that tipped the balance and allowed his greed to overwhelm his fears. The impetus came when Grayling gained access to the Sites and Monuments register. Here he found maps, dozens of wonderful detailed maps which recorded every find, every earthwork and site of archaeological note in the county. The copies he had made of these maps had led him to every site that he had missed in the area although, as with all his previous excursions, he singularly failed to find anything of any great monetary value. But when he came to study the map which included the parish of Stoches he saw, for the first time, that the benighted mound on the edge of the village was far more than just the base of an old gallows or the footings for a mill. According to the notes on the maps, the Gallows Grave was nothing less than a Neolithic round barrow, the burial mound of some prehistoric noble who would undoubtedly, as far as Grayling was concerned, have been buried with great ceremony and even greater treasure. When he saw that note all his fears were forgotten and he determined that, as soon as possible, he would take his detector and search the mound for the treasure he knew would rightfully soon be his.

So it was that, on one cold, clear November night, Bobby Grayling and his semi-moronic cousin Ronny set out from Fernbank to walk the path out to the old road. From there they cut across into the fields to avoid being spotted by travellers in their vehicles. It was a clear night and finding their way through the hedges proved little obstacle to their progress so that, within the hour and with the clock standing at just before one in the morning, that found themselves stood on the edge of the field looking across at the Gallows Grave. The field was ploughed, tilled and planted with winter wheat which appeared as a green fur some four inches in height, coating the dark soil beneath. There was a fine sheen of frost across the whole field and there, barely visible on the far side was the grass covered mound of Gallows Grave.

-

Early in his life Bobby had decided he needed a nickname, something that set him out as an individual, a man apart from those poor saps who spent their days in toil and their nights in fitful sleep. After much thought he had settled upon the name Otter. An Otter was a sleek, quick-witted animal, handsome, elusive, a hunter; all the things that Bobby imagined to be part of his character. Of course, simply deciding you wanted a nickname was not enough. You had to convince people to use it as well. This was all the more difficult when, as in Bobby's case, those who knew him saw him as more of a toad than an otter.

As it turned out, the only person who could be persuaded to use the nickname was Ronny and that was only after he had been bribed with large quantities of Dolly Mixtures. If one could forget his extreme idiocy for a moment, then these sweets were Ronny's one great weakness and Grayling always ensured he had a twist or three in his pocket to guarantee his cousin's unquestioning obedience. It was times like this, stood on the edge of a frosted field in the small hours of the morning looking over at a reputedly haunted burial mound, that Grayling was thankful for the lack of imagination in his moronic relation. Give Ronny enough sweets and his brain melted in the sugar rush so that he would obey the most ludicrous of instructions without the slightest hesitation – well, no more than was normal for him anyway.

"Wah we doin' Otter?" Ronny asked through a mouth full of half chewed fondant.

"What we are doing, dear cousin, is making ourselves rich." As he replied, Grayling never took his eyes off the mound that lay shrouded in darkness on the extreme limits of his vision. Even on a night like this, with the constellations clear in the sky and the Milky Way a soft white blur across the heavens, the Gallows Grave seemed to generate its own deep shadow in which it lurked menacingly.

"Pick up the bags and follow me Ronny. We're going to do a bit of digging."

They set forth across the field towards the mound, watching all the while for signs of movement on the road or lights in the houses a few dozen yards away on the edge of the village. More than once in his short career as a nighthawk, Grayling had been forced to flee after falling foul of a nosy neighbour or an observant police patrol. They had never caught him yet but Bobby had learned that, even in the most unlikely of circumstances, he should always keep half an eye on the lookout for the authorities.

Grayling spent the next hour sweeping the field close to the barrow, listening intently for the squeaks and whines in his earphones that would indicate the presence of metal. A good nighthawk could even tell what sort of metal he was detecting, by the tone of the feedback from the detector and the flick of the needle on the dial set into the handle of the machine. And although he had only been detecting a few years, Grayling was very, very good. This night he knew what he was after and it wasn't iron. Most of the time, iron turned out to be horseshoe nails or bits of old farm machinery, rusted slices of ploughshare and twisted pieces of threshing machine. This night particularly, Bobby wasn't going to waste time on those. He was here for treasure and that meant gold, silver or bronze. Although the grave itself dated from the late Neolithic and so, in spite of Grayling's daydreams, was unlikely to contain anything of real value as far as treasure was concerned, Grayling knew from his books that later peoples, particularly in the Bronze Age and much later in the Saxon period, had held these mounds in great veneration and had often reused them for burying their own dead. If he was lucky here was every chance of finding Bronze Age weapons or a Saxon hoard hastily buried to hide it from the approaching Danes.

But after an hour, with Grayling straining to pick up even the slightest trace of hidden metal, nothing of any value had been uncovered. He pulled the headphones from his ears for a moment and looked about him. Ronny sat on the lower slopes of the mound facing the road, watching for cars and clutching his spade in anticipation of digging to be done once Grayling indicated he had something worth investigating. He was cold, the frosted ground was damp through his trousers and, having finished his twist of dolly mixtures, he was feeling more than a little rebellious.

"What we doin' Otter?" he asked for the second time that night.

"I've already told you Ronny. We are looking for treasure." Grayling snapped back.

"Have we found any yet?"

"Does it look like it you idiot? Now shut up and let me think for a minute?"

Ronny looked at his cousin for a moment and then asked the obvious question. "Why haven't you looked on the mound, Otter? I would 'ave thought that the treasure would be buried in the mound. Doncha think we should look in the mound?"

Grayling reflected that his cousin was right of course. The mound was the obvious place to look. He had convinced himself that by checking the area around the mound first he was just being thorough but he knew that, in truth, what he was really doing was just delaying the moment when he had to step upon that grassy knoll. If there was any treasure to be found it was upon that mound and there was no longer any reason for putting off his search of it.

He advanced to the edge of the plough soil close to where Ronny sat, and stood for a moment looking at the barrow. He told himself it was just a mound of earth. He knew that was all it was. A pile of soil covering the remains of a man that had been dead for four thousand years. But still… there was something. He remembered old Gibbet John who had disappeared somewhere in this field. He remembered the stories of the creaking beam and the fear he had felt as a child every time he had to walk past this place.

And then he looked down at Ronny. Simple Ronny, sat there on the mound without a care in the world - except perhaps that his toes might fall off if they stayed out in this field much longer. Happy Ronny, if you ignored the cold, hoping that Grayling might reach into his pocket and bring out another of those twists of dolly mixtures. Grayling laughed at his own stupid superstition and, reaching into his pocket to make Ronny happy, he stepped forward onto the grass.

The ground was softer than he had expected but, as he passed the sweets to his cousin and took another step up the slope, he concluded that this was just an illusion as a result of stepping off the hard, frozen soil of the field and onto the springy grass of the mound. He continued to climb the barrow.

It should have taken no more than eight or ten steps to reach the summit but, as he approached the crest, Grayling realised that he did not seem to be as high as he expected. The ground appeared to be very soft indeed, almost like he was walking through a patch of deep mud. He turned to look back at his cousin still sat at the base of the barrow and as he did, he heard the unmistakeable creak of an old wooden beam, straining under a heavy swinging load.

Bobby gasped and looked down at his feet. He was less than two yards from the top of the mound but now, as he regarded the ground, he realised that he had sunk up to his knees into the earth of the Gallows Grave. He tried to lift his leg, but the soil seemed to grip his ankle and prevented him from pulling his foot free. The sound of the beam creaking in the wind grew ever louder. Yet there was no wind.

Now Grayling was truly terrified, more frightened than he had ever been in his miserable life. He threw his detector down the slope towards his cousin and gave an anguished cry.

"Ronny!! Help, help me. I'm sinking, something's got my foot Ronny, help me!"

For the first time, Ronny became aware that something was wrong. He jumped up from the mound and, stepping back onto the plough soil, looked up at his cousin sinking slowly into the top of the barrow.

"Wha… whatcha doin Otter? Whats happenin?"

"Help me you idiot, something's got my foot. Its dragging me down, for Christ's sake help meee..."

Ronny had already started up the mound towards his stricken cousin but as he heard Grayling's shouts and realised that this wasn't just a hole that his cousin had fallen into, that he had actually been seized by something beneath the ground, he stopped and started to back away down to the foot of the barrow. In the distance he could hear the creak of a tree bending in the wind and, though he had no idea what it might mean, he knew it frightened him. And he knew that there was no wind.

Grayling had now sunk up to his chest and the tight grip was moving inexorably up his body. The creaking had now risen in volume to the point where he could hardly hear his own voice as he cried out in desperation to his cousin, who was backing further and further away into the darkness, a look of terrified horror on his face.

"Ronny!! Ron..." the soil came up over his chin and flowed into his mouth, choking back the scream that tried to burst from Grayling's lips. Then it was over his nose and he was being sucked down through the grass into the darkness of the Gallows Grave.

As Bobby's head finally disappeared beneath the ground and the creaking of the gallows faded away into the still silent November night, Ronny did the only think that any intelligent man would do. He turned and fled. He fled right out of the field, out of the village and out of the county. He was never seen again in the parish of Fernbank.

-

With the flight of Ronny, the fate of Bobby Grayling should have remained one of those mysteries never to be solved. His wife reported him missing but was generally unconcerned by his disappearance, assuming that he had probably 'done a runner' with a barmaid from one of the town centre pubs. It was certainly not unheard of and would be entirely in keeping with his character. Mrs Grayling had enough money in the bank to keep her happy and was sure that Bobby would turn up again sooner or later.

"Probably sooner, more's the pity."

But by strange chance it was less than a month before the mystery of what had become of the nighthawk was solved. And in the resolution of one mystery there invariably lie the seeds of many more. In this case those seeds soon sprouted into a whole forest of confusion.

It had been known for some time that the old Roman road was in need of improvement. The growth of Aldwark as a town and the need for people to travel into the city for work meant that there were simply too many vehicles on the road. So it was decided that a bright, big new road should be built parallel to, but some distance from, the original. As is traditional practice in these matters, even though it would still be some years before the building began, it was further decided that any archaeological features along the route should be investigated to ensure that nothing of any import would be destroyed by the wide strip of asphalt that would soon be sweeping north east across the previously undisturbed farmland. Of course, given its prominence in the area, one of the first sites to be targeted by the archaeologists was the Gallows Grave. As it lay very close to the proposed route and there was every chance that it might be destroyed during the road building, it was decided that an excavation would be undertaken to ascertain if the local myths were true and there really was a tomb at the centre. That excavation started less than a fortnight after Bobby Grayling had disappeared on the barrow.

The excavators were dedicated and professional in their task. Everything was recorded, sectioned, drawn and photographed in meticulous detail. Every sherd of pottery was cleaned and studied for clues about its age. Every flake of flint was examined to identify those that had been worked. Soil was sieved, scraps of wood and leather were whisked away to the university for conservation, tiny animal bones, shells and husks of grain were all preserved for later analysis. And then, just over a week after they had begun digging, the archaeologists came upon the proof they had been looking for. As the soil and turf was stripped away from the top of the mound, a large cap stone, twice the size of a man, was revealed resting across the top of a stone lined chamber – a prehistoric tomb. Further excavation, again with photographs and drawings at every stage, revealed that the tomb consisted of three large upright megaliths capped with a fourth. Unusually perhaps, it was sealed as tight as could be, with every gap between the larger stones filled with smaller rocks and pieces of rubble to make an almost airtight chamber.

There was much debate over the next few days about the best way to remove the stones, and it was eventually decided to remove some of the smaller material, to allow a crane to be brought in, and a hawser passed through the chamber to secure the cap stone which could then be lifted out to reveal the insides of the tomb. This was duly accomplished and the whole team gathered around the stone chamber to witness the lifting of the capstone and to catch a glimpse of what was revealed within. It was a moment none of them would ever forget.

-

The police were, of course, involved. But an interview with Ronny, who was found hiding in a seedy guest house in Chester, left them just as bewildered as when they had first examined the scene. Specialist forensic experts were enlisted, the most eminent archaeologists were consulted. Every photograph, drawing and note was examined in minute detail. But at every turn the conclusions were the same. Prior to the removal of the huge capstone by the archaeology team, the tomb had remained undisturbed since the last days of the Neolithic some four thousand years before.

Once all the police investigations were completed, the coroner had to make some attempt to produce a verdict that would fit the extraordinary circumstances. There were simply so many questions left unanswered, so many impossibilities, that even the open verdict that was eventually passed down hardly seemed to do justice to the downright weirdness of the case.

The facts were simple enough. When the capstone was removed from the tomb, within there lay the remains of three people. The first, now reduced to a series of neatly stacked bones in one corner of the chamber in the tradition of his ancient culture, had been dead at least four thousand years. The second, also little more than bones in a shroud of rags and leather fittings, had apparently been a man of some importance judging by the rings on his fingers and the money in his pouch. These effects would later help his remains to be dated to the late eighteenth century, and a trawl of the records would allow the coroner to tentatively suggest the connection between this skeleton and the long lost 4th Earl, Gibbet John.

The last man, his fingers bloody and torn where they had clawed at the stones, had been dead just under four weeks and otherwise bore not a mark of injury nor exhibited any sign of decomposition. Cause of death was determined as heart failure, but no autopsy could determine how long Grayling had lain in that unbroken, unending, impenetrable darkness before he finally succumbed to the terror. A broken penknife was found lying alongside the body and, as one of the diggers later observed, the underside of the capstone bore the scars of a desperate, futile attempt by the wretched man to scratch his way out through twenty-five tons of solid rock that had not been moved in more than four millennia.

What the coroner did not record in his verdict, and what would cause him many a sleepless night for the rest of his long life, was a short note inscribed amongst the papers of the 4th Earl, relating to the last man he condemned to the gallows before he himself disappeared from the world of men. He found the papers whilst trying to unearth some explanation, any explanation, for the mystery of the bodies in the Gallows Grave. What he found gave him little comfort.

"I curse these ignorant brutes who come before me daily. They serve no useful purpose and refuse to accept their station in life, their place in the natural order of things. Would that the ground itself might open up and swallow them, every last one of them and save me the trouble and expense of their trial.

Any man who would stand against his rightful master, any low criminal who would kill and steal and lust and break God's commands deserves no better than to be sucked straight down into hell without so much as a stone to mark his passing.

A curse on them all. Let the cold earth have them."

Black Dog

English folklore abounds with tales of spectral hellhounds with apparently as many different names as there are sightings of the beasts. Traditionally they are considered to be portents of death and there are few parts of the country that do not have their own particular version of the tale, some more fearsome than others.

One thing that tends to be lacking from most of these tales is any explanation as to the origins of the ghostly dogs. They are simply an accepted part of the supernatural landscape. So with this story I sought to explore one possible origin for these apparitions by linking the manifestations with Winston Churchill's famous and evocative description of his depressive episodes.

For me the other appealing element of this story is the idea of a community that accepts the supernatural as simply another part of their daily lives, the idea that folklore has been so inculcated into their psyche that they accept the paranormal without question as a natural part of their existence. This is surely not so far from reality for most people even in our own supposedly rational modern societies.

Black Dog

Robert Thorneycroft was a deeply troubled man.

By his thirtieth birthday he had, to his own mind at least, achieved nothing of worth in his life. To be sure he had a job, a good one at that, with a small accounting firm in the local town. He was well thought of and prospects were good, his colleagues would say very good. He had his own house; a cottage on the edge of the picturesque village of Scarthorpe with views from the back looking out across the fields and up onto the heath beyond. He had a close-knit group of friends, both male and female, who provided company – good company with no pressure but which ensured he need never be lonely either by day or night. He had security, income, companionship and a future. In most people's eyes his was a life to be envied.

But as he approached his fourth decade it dawned upon Thorneycroft that so far, by his own reckoning, he was a failure. No, worse than that, he had not even attempted anything which could be weighed against the scales of success and failure. He had done nothing that he considered of value with his life. He had made no mark, not even a smudge on the record of worldly achievement. Were he to pass from life that very evening of his birthday he would do so having left absolutely nothing worthwhile behind. At least that was his own, admittedly rather dramatic, assessment of his life to date.

He would often consider that, in contrast, by the time he reached the celebration of his thirtieth year his father had created a successful newspaper business, had built with his own two hands his own house in a pleasant village on the outskirts of Aldwark, and was well on the way to raising two children who, it had been hoped, would be a credit to their parents. All these were worthwhile and valuable achievements. They may not exactly have been the things that the younger Thorneycroft dreamed of, but he recognised their value. The foundation of a family home and the perpetuation of the line into the future were, by any standards, achievements to be proud of, but when it came right down to it they were not the ambitions that would ever and could ever drive the son in the way they had the father.

With all his heart and all his soul, Thorneycroft was an aspiring writer. He thought a pretty good one at that. He also liked to think he was an idealist. He wrote not for money – although of course a little supplement to his income would not have been unwelcome. He wrote not for fame... well at least not for the sort of fame that most people considered worthwhile pursuing these days. What he wrote for, what he desired more than anything, was immortality. Not physical, he had no great faith in either religion or science to provide the answers to that one in his lifetime. What he craved was more philosophical. He wanted to leave behind something 'of value'; something that would mean that, a hundred years from now, even though he would be long gone from this land, he would still be remembered. He wanted to make his mark and he wanted it to be carved in the literary equivalent of granite. This had been his overriding ambition since his school days, and it was a fire that had only burned ever more fiercely as year after year he found himself trapped in the mundane existence of daily life. What had started as frustration had long ago taken a hold on his soul and metamorphosed into deep resentment and, most recently, depression.

The resentment was not at those around him. He begrudged no one their success and would not have had a bad word to say about anyone who had achieved what he so desperately yearned for. All his anger and resentment was directed inward, towards himself. He clearly saw his own limitations, his own failings. His thirtieth birthday was, of course, just another day. But to the frustrated artist it symbolised the worthlessness of his existence. He saw stretching before him a life bereft of meaning or achievement, a life whose ending would have no greater import for the wider world than had its beginning. And so, as the days passed and the mundane continued to smother him, Thorneycroft slumped deeper and deeper into the black pit of despair. His friends tried to help, to lift him from his torpor, but in truth they little understood the reason for his depression and so, perhaps sooner than their avowed loyalty would have dictated, they abandoned the writer, finding other bars at which to drink, other fires in front of which to sit and chat.

And so, each evening Thorneycroft found himself alone with his thoughts on a bench in a dark corner of the *Stone Stool.* He was already a familiar figure in the pub but now, bereft of his friends, for the first time the locals saw the change in his demeanour. Their attempts to draw him into the light met with little success and eventually they chose to leave him nursing his ale under a wide, black cloud. Inevitably, as the summer drew to a close and the nights darkened into autumn and then winter, the whispered comments and gossip began. They did not, you might be surprised to hear, dwell long on the reasons for the writer's depression. For the regulars of the *Stone Stool,* cause was really of little concern. What bothered them more was effect.

Joe Chartman, a small, gaunt-faced, local farmer who made his living growing peas for grocers and markets across three counties, was the first to articulate the fear that had grown in them all over the weeks.

"He should be careful, that one, or else he'll end up bringing the Shucca down on us."

"The Shucca?" The question came from Andy Braith, a young farmhand from the far side of the county, over for one of the darts matches which were regular fixtures between the country pubs.

Joe's brother Fred piped up.

"Ay, old Hairy Jack himself. When the blackness takes a man this close to the Hope, it's only a matter of time before the Shucca comes a calling. Mark my word, there'll be deaths in the village before the week is done."

'The Hope' was the local name for the high heath which lay to the east of the Jurassic limestone scarp on which Scarthorpe stood. Its name was a corruption of the old Saxon word *Hoep* which meant literally 'heath'. The Saxon roots ran deep in the villages and hamlets which dotted the length of the escarpment and this was reflected in many of the local place names.

The farmhand smiled broadly. "Come on, Mr Chartman. You're sounding like an extra from a cheap Hammer film. You're an educated man, not some local yokel. You don't really believe all those stories do you? They are just what we tell the kids to stop them wandering off after dark or straying too far onto the heath, so we don't end up having to go looking for them when the mist comes down. But no one actually believes it all do they?"

His last question was directed at the bar as a whole, and as he finished he turned out towards his fellow drinkers looking for expected support. What he got was a dozen or more men and women looking straight back at him with a mixture of pity and amusement.

Andy Braith looked confused. "You have to be joking. Are you telling me everyone in this room actually believes these ghost stories? You're having me on, aren't you?"

It was Joe Chartman who answered. "Who said anything about belief, Andy. We don't have to believe. There isn't a soul who has lived in this village more than twenty years who hasn't seen the Shucca – not face to face mind, but still just as clear as the harvest moon on a late September night. The Shucca isn't a myth or a fairy story, Andy. It's as real as you or I. We know. We've seen it. We've chased shadows down the back lane and out on to the Hope for fear that it would take one of the children. We've buried the men and women who brought it down upon us, and while we prayed for their souls and grieved for their loss, at the same time a part of us has been thanking God that their deaths have brought an end to the fear, at least for a while. The Shucca is real, Andy. Never doubt that."

Another voice spoke up from the end of the bar. "Ay, and it's the black thoughts of the likes of him," he nodded in the direction of the far corner table where Thorneycroft sat alone, drowning in his ale, "that will bring the beast back to the village again."

Joe looked across for a moment at the writer and then back at his own pint pot.

"We'll see," he said quietly, "we'll see."

It was only two days later that the deaths began.

Scarthorpe was one of the lucky few villages which had retained a local post office whilst the government seemed to be intent on shutting down every last one of them across the rest of the shires. In part, this might have been due to the fact that there was no regular postman for the village and the post was dropped off in a bundle at the post office to be collected by the villagers as they passed by. This arrangement suited most of the inhabitants as the post office also served as the local shop and garage so there was always some reason to be popping down.

There were a few however, who were unable or unwilling to make the trip and preferred to have their mail delivered to their doorstep. Bob Foreman was one such, confined to his cottage up on the edge of the Hope for the last twelve years, as age took its toll on his creaking frame. If letters or parcels should arrive for Bob then the postmistress, Mrs Marshall, would scoop them up, put a note on the door and drive her old Escort car the mile or so up the lane for a cup of tea and a chat with the old man.

When they found the car it was sat in the middle of the lane with the engine still running and the windscreen wipers were still squeaking back and forth. It was a wet sort of day, low cloud merging with high mist to form a damp blanket which enveloped the land, soaking everything in minutes. Joe Chartman had arrived at the post office perhaps an hour after Mrs Marshall had put the note on the door. After waiting for fifteen minutes or so he had developed a sudden and irrational fear and had decided to take his Land Rover up to Bob Foreman's cottage, 'just in case'. When he reached the Ford, the driver's side door was still open, and the seat was sodden where the misting rain had drifted down upon it. Susan Marshall lay crumpled in the road a few yards beyond the front of the car. There was no mark upon her body. Her wet clothes were otherwise undamaged and there was no sign of a struggle or any form of assault upon the unfortunate lady.

The other things that the farmer saw, as he waited for the ambulance, he saw no point in reporting to the authorities. Long before it was announced as the official cause of death, he knew that Susan Marshall's heart had failed. He knew too that with a verdict of 'natural causes', no one outside of the village would be interested in the look of sheer terror that had masked the victim's face as he gently closed her eyes for the last time. Nor would they have any reason to take an interest in the two large paw prints he found in the mud close to the edge of the road near where the body lay. Taken in the right way these clues could lead to a conclusion that the death was anything but natural but Joe knew that, outside of his small, tight-knit community, no one would consider his ideas as anything more than wild superstition. So he kept his council and saved it for the only audience he knew would be receptive to his words.

Though if Joe Chartman had hoped to prevent further death, time and the beast were both against him. The very next night, before he had a chance to put his thoughts to his neighbours, the great black dog paid a second visit to Scarthorpe. Though Joe had had no chance to speak formally to his friends, all those who dwelt in the village could sense that something was amiss, and those who were familiar with the history of the place had a good idea as to the reason for the air of unease that settled over the rooftops that late October night. They had the good sense to make sure the youngest children were in bed, the doors bolted and the heavy winter curtains shut tight against the darkness, long before the church clock struck six. The streets were empty and an unnatural silence descended upon the village.

Robert Thorneycroft was sat in his small study staring at the few, meaningless lines he had managed to tap away on the typewriter over the last hour and a half. His mind was a blank. He had moved beyond that melange of useless plotless thoughts that normally characterised his writers block. Now his head was empty of all thought except black, paralysing despair. Eventually he decided he was thirsty. He would get a drink. That was, at least, something positive he could do. A cup of tea. That would at least have the benefit of warming his cold, stiff fingers which seemed to have frozen as completely as his mind.

He arose and walked through the lounge into the small kitchen. He took the kettle and stood at the sink, staring out of the window into the damp, dank, autumn night, whilst it slowly filled with water. The small kitchen window had been left ajar and a breath of cold, wet air drifted into the house through the narrow gap along the sill. Thorneycroft guessed that this was a good explanation for the chill that had infected his bones and, cursing his stupidity, he put the kettle down on the draining board and reached over to pull the sash down.

It was then that he saw it.

Dog was not so insufficient a word to describe the great beast that stood on the track just outside his back gate. This was a hound, the likes of which he could not have imagined in even his worst nightmares. Black as coal dust, larger than a small pony, its wet, red lips drawn back to reveal a mouth filled with diamond sharp teeth. The large, elongated canines dripping with a dark viscous liquid that could only be the blood of some recently riven creature, which the writer fervently hoped had not been human.

In the still, otherwise silent, autumnal night air he could hear the persistent, low, gravelling growl from deep within the back of the creature's throat. He could see the clouds of hot breath that momentarily shrouded its head every time it exhaled.

Thorneycroft froze with his hand grasping the bottom of the window. He knew from experience that if he pulled it down the noise would be loud enough to alert the hound to his presence. For now it was looking away, down towards the new houses that had been built on the old mill site at the bottom of the village. But he knew that if he made the slightest sound then the eyes of that terrible beast, eyes he could only imagine as bottomless burning pits, would fix upon him and burn out his very soul. Slowly, oh so terribly slowly, he withdrew his hand and sank to the floor below the sink.

For a dozen, glacial minutes he crouched there, not daring to raise his head to see if the beast still lurked at the end of his garden. Only when the urge to relieve himself became overpowering did he risk glancing over the taps and out into the garden. The path was empty. Whatever the creature had been that had paused by his gate, whatever had caused it to hesitate at that particular spot, it had now moved on. He hoped forever, he feared otherwise.

More fearful than he ever remembered feeling in all his life, Robert Thorneycroft retreated to his bed and lay out the night, unsleeping, the sheets drawn tight up to his chin and his eyes fixed hard upon the curtains, awaiting the gradual lightening of the world which he hoped would bring an end to his terror.

In the light of a soggy autumn morning the village seemed a dour, sullen place, resisting all attempts to drag it into the day. Lonely figures scuttled along pavements between house, shop and bus stop, eyes fixed to the ground, faces hardened to a blank mask. It was as if the whole community had become infected with Thorneycroft's black mood.

And as the day progressed, while Thorneycroft sat at his desk in Aldwark and tried to drive the images of the previous night from his mind, the latest news only brought further despair upon the village. Following hard on the heels of the death of the postmistress, two more souls had departed the world overnight.

James Phipps, the retired headmaster from the local infants, had suffered a stroke, apparently whilst trying to close the curtains in his back bedroom which looked out onto the Hope, a few doors along from Thorneycroft's cottage. He was found by his daughter the following morning, slumped below the window, wrapped in the curtains he had dragged down as he fell.

More tragic still was the death of Caitlin Jennings, a single mother who lived with her twins in one of the Millside Estate houses that had spread the village far beyond its original boundaries. On that dreadful evening she had left the children with her mother as she prepared for her weekly match with the *Stone Stool* Ladies Darts Team over at the *Otter's Rest* in Fernbank. It seems she had been tidying away the children's toys which were scattered across the back lawn, when she had been surprised by something or someone that caused her to take fright and stumble back towards the house, tripping over a carelessly parked scooter and falling to catch the back of her head on the kitchen step. She died instantly.

Neither death would raise any suspicion with the police or coroner. The question of what had caused Miss Jennings to stumble backwards so violently away from the rear gate was considered briefly by the local police liaison officer but, since there were no other suspicious circumstances, there was no reason to pursue the matter further. The three deaths in two days were considered nothing more than an unfortunate coincidence and the arrangements were made for the funerals.

But those who had lived longest in the village knew that there was more than mere coincidence in the fatalities and that, if they were to prevent further untimely deaths, something very specific would have to be done.

As befits events of such import, the meeting was held in the lounge bar of the *Stone Stool*. Whilst visitors and 'newcomers' were restricted to the main bar that Thursday evening, a private conference of villagers was held next door to discuss what were circumspectly referred to as 'matters'.

The thirty or so people gathered in the lounge all knew the ultimate reason for the meeting and all, it appeared, were of a mind when it came to what had to be done.

"It has to stop. We have to stop it now."

The well-fed lady of indeterminate middle age, sat at a table close to the large, stone built fire-place, was clearly used to being obeyed without question but this evening there was the slight hint of hysteria in her voice.

"We will Mrs Cartwright, we will. Rest assured there will be no more unnecessary deaths in the village."

As the man who had called this meeting, Joe Chartman - propped up with his back against the bar, flanked by his brother and one of his farmhands - had naturally assumed the position of chairman. He intended to make sure that everyone remained focused and that the matters at hand were dealt with quickly and, more importantly, in the manner that he believed best served the whole village. He knew what had to be done, as, he suspected, did most of the others present. But there were sure to be one or two who balked at taking the necessary action and he intended to make sure they were dealt with quickly and ruthlessly lest they persuade others to turn aside from the difficult decision at hand.

"The first step it seems to me," said John Wiseman in low, measured tones, the result of many years practice as a solicitor in Aldwark, "is to make sure we agreed as to the cause of this problem. I know it is a hard fact to face, but does anyone here defer from the sad but necessary opinion that young Mr Thorneycroft is ultimately the source of this present crisis?"

Looking round the room, Chartman could see that there were one or two who dearly wished to speak up and oppose this contention but that, in truth, all knew John Wiseman's statement to be correct.

Chartman decided to take charge. He knew that the mood of the room was such, that a bit of leadership at the right moment would cut short any unnecessary discussion and draw out the right decision. The villagers were all frightened and, much as they might hate themselves for it, they knew there was only one way in which their fears would be resolved. It was Chartman's job, as he saw it, to cut through the concerns and lead them to the proper conclusion.

"So, if we are all agreed on the reason for this sorry state of affairs, are we also agreed that there is only one course of action left open to us?"

Though phrased as a question, everyone in the room knew that the farmer was making a clear statement of intent and was challenging anyone to disagree.

John Wiseman's wife, Diana, spoke up. "Can we at least try talking to the boy? See if there is anything to be done to bring him to his senses? After all he is just depressed. We all get depressed sometimes. It doesn't last forever."

"You know as well as I do that there is little point in that, Di. We should have realised sooner that Thorneycroft was slipping into depression and we could have taken the appropriate action then. We have all been in the same situation and we have relied on each other to make sure that anyone affected leaves the village until they have dealt with the problems and it is safe to return. We simply took our eye off the ball this time. Of course I am sure that Reverend Travers," Chartman nodded in the direction of the vicar sat on a stool at the end of the bar, cradling a large glass of Calvados, "will see what he can do to rectify the situation, but for myself I really don't hold out much hope now that the beast is on the hunt again."

The vicar took this as his cue to make his own contribution to the discussion.

"Well you all know my feelings on the matter. The church was built with a purpose and has served this village well through the centuries. I see no reason to start second guessing things now. Particularly given that we have had three deaths in very short order and we know there will be more. This matter is in the hands of the Lord and St Hubert. Let the church do what it is there for and let that be an end to it."

"I, of course, will have a chat with the lad, invite him over to the church so we can do a bit of research and put him in the picture. See what comes of it. I am sure it will all work out in the end so long as we are firm in our resolve."

Chartman was glad that Travers was there. A tall, well-built man with a clipped turn of phrase who was never to be seen out and about in anything but his best, the vicar had always given the impression of being the pragmatic sort of churchman, the sort that made good military padres; a 'praise the lord and pass the ammunition' sort of chap. He knew what had to be done and would not hesitate in what he saw as his duty, both to the village and to the church.

It was clear that, despite many understandable reservations, there was no one in the room who was willing to raise any real objections. They all had families who could very easily be the next ones to fall victim to the beast. No one can be too high-minded about their morals when the lives of their children are at risk. The fact that the vicar appeared to hold no doubts clearly helped to sway the mood firmly towards action and Chartman decided to wrap things up before people had a chance to think things through too deeply.

"Now you all know how this works, so we won't go into the details here. There is nothing for you to do but make sure you keep yourselves and your families safe for the next twenty-four hours. It is the weekend coming up so perhaps it is a good time to consider visiting relatives. Or if not – I saw you wince, Jack, so don't worry, we won't force you to go to your mother-in-law's – then why not get the kids over to their grandparents and go out for a night in Aldwark. Just make sure that whatever you do you are not out after dark tomorrow night. And stay off the Hope. That goes for everyone."

He looked round at the faces filled with fear, hope and perhaps still a little guilt.

"Don't worry folks. By Sunday morning this will all be over."

There were a few nods, a few sad shakes of the head and that was it. Bill Vickers, the landlord who had overseen the proceedings from beside the hatch, behind the bar where he kept a weather eye to customers in the other room, came forward and began pulling pints – on the house for this evening. Chartman picked up his whisky and moved across to the end of the bar where the vicar was sat, lost in thought.

"So how will you approach this?"

"Well, as providence would have it – ours rather than his of course – Thorneycroft is sat through in the corner of the main bar right now, nursing his pint. I have a sneaking suspicion that he had a fright last night and I thought this might be an opportune moment for me to go through and have a word with him."

"If you need any help with... well, with anything, you only have to ask."

"Oh I know Joe, I know. I will be fine. After all its not the first time is it."

"No, true. But I do keep hoping each time that it might be the last."

Robert Thorneycroft sat quietly in the corner of the bar and stared into his pint. It had become a familiar position for him over the last few months, but tonight his thoughts were far removed from those that had occupied his mind since the late summer. The terrifying experience of the previous evening had wrought a fundamental change in the man. His depression was gone, driven from his mind first by a numbing fear. But then, as the fear receded with the coming of the dawn, it had been replaced not by a return to indolent despair, but by a burning curiosity, a desperate desire to find out what it was he had seen the previous night. He had no doubt that its origins were supernatural. He even had a fair idea of the nature of the creature, being aware of the legends of great black dogs which presaged death to those who looked into their burning red eyes; eyes, if his childhood books were to be believed, the size of dinner plates.

But the experience had reinvigorated him. So it was that whilst, to all outward appearances, the young writer was still lost in the fog of depression, in fact his whole outlook on life had been transformed. He saw in this fascinating incident the opportunity for a whole series of finely wrought stories, tales of midnight terror that would make both his name and his fortune. Not those crass horror stories that modern writers seemed to churn out endlessly; all blood and dismemberment. No, these would-be classics, in the style of M.R. James or Sheridan Le Fanu. Stories to tell one another in hushed tones, in front of a great log fire on stormy winter nights. For the first time in months Thorneycroft smiled. He could do it, he knew he could.

"Good evening Mr Thorneycroft. May I join you?"

Shaken from his thoughts by the unexpected interruption, Robert looked up from his ale to see the tall figure of the Vicar stood before him on the other side of the wooden table.

"Err, yes, yes of course vicar. Please, sit down."

"I apologise for disturbing you in your meditations this evening. I understand things have been a little... difficult for you lately. If you would prefer to be alone...?"

"No, no, that's fine. I was just thinking about a story I plan to write."

Thorneycroft's unexpected smile surprised Travers, momentarily distracting him from his planned approach.

"Yes, I see. I had heard that you were a writer. So what particular subject has inspired you this evening?"

And so Thorneycroft sat and, hesitantly at first, fearful at discussing something so extraordinary with a man of the cloth, told his story to a surprisingly receptive Reverend Travers.

By the end of the evening the writer and the vicar, now on first name terms, parted with a promise to meet again the following evening at the church. The vicar had, he said, some very interesting books and papers relating to the sightings of great dogs in the villages surrounding the Hope, which he was sure would be of interest to the younger man.

"The people round here, they've stayed connected with the past a little more than most. With the old words and the old ways."

Thorneycroft and Reverend Travers were stood side by side in front of an old leather topped desk, in a small room half hidden off to one side of the altar, in Scarthorpe's ancient church of St Hubert's. The vicar had just retrieved a number of volumes from a large, glass-fronted bookcase and was studying the spines in search of one particular book.

"Now where are we? Ah yes, here we are. As I was saying, the tales of this supernatural hound are positively abound in the villages around the Hope. They have various names for him but most commonly he is known as the Shucca, at least that is the name I have heard used most often in my time here."

He studied a small blue volume he had picked out from the pile.

"They do say – I do love that turn of phrase you know, so country yokel – as I was saying, they do say, that the dog is searching... searching for the poor troubled soul that created it. And that when he finds him, no more will be seen of either man or dog."

"Created it? How? Is this something like an experiment gone wrong?"

"Oh, no no, you misunderstand. The story goes that the Shucca is a creation of the Hope itself. The heath, the wooded vales, the rivers and streams, the land itself, they judge a man. They judge him based not upon their ideas of worth, but upon his own. They are a mirror for his own perceptions of success and failure. The story goes that the Shucca is created by a mood of black despair; it is, if you like, desolation incarnate, misery-made manifest. Hmm, I rather like that last one," he chuckled, "pleasingly alliterative."

Thorneycroft prompted the older man to continue.

"Yes, yes, as I was saying, it is all in this little book you see. Well, maybe not all, but a fair bit of it anyway. In the summer of 1863, the then vicar of St Hubert's began to investigate the Black Dog that had plagued his parish down the centuries. Reverend Tomkins – that was his name of course – spent the autumn and winter of that year trawling the archives and talking with anyone in the village who claimed to have any knowledge of the beast. As a result, in the following spring, he produced a small book – this very one – which was published by a local printers in Aldwark. A fascinating read it was and quite popular in the county. But unfortunately the Bishop was not amused. He considered it to be unseemly for a man of the cloth to be seen to be giving credence to what he called 'childish local superstitions'. He said it was tantamount to dabbling in the occult. When the good reverend was asked to explain his actions and chose instead to try to defend both the book and the legends, the Bishop had him replaced."

He passed the slim volume over to Thorneycroft.

"Here, borrow this for a while and have a read. Hopefully it will help you with your story."

There was a kettle at the back of the room and Travers reached over and flicked the switch before turning towards the door.

"Come along with me for a minute. We will need a cup of tea if we are to stay here for long, heaven knows it's a cold old night. While we are waiting for it to boil there are a couple of things I would like to show you."
Thorneycroft slipped the book into his pocket and followed out into the aisle where the vicar was already continuing his story.

"Poor old Tomkins. It is thought he himself fell victim to the beast only the following year. After the Bishop removed him from his post he took to wandering the

Hope. Perhaps looking for the hound, perhaps just finding consolation in the great outdoors. Who knows. He was certainly a broken man and, as I mentioned, it seems the beast has a particular affinity for troubled minds. He disappeared one October evening after heading out along the ridge path towards Engcaster."

"I still don't understand what you said about someone creating the hound. Is it just a figment of the imagination then?"

"Oh no, no, no. No, it is as real as you or I, at least for a while anyway. The belief in these parts is that the spectral dog is a result of the interaction between the Hope and troubled minds. Whether for punishment or some other unknown reason, they believe that if someone is suffering under a malevolent mood then the hound comes forth to hunt them down. Like most of these stories it is believed that anyone whose path is crossed by the beast will suffer some terrible fate. That bit varies from place to place around the country. Either they are taken then and there, or they will die within so many days, or something terrible will befall a loved one. No two tales are exactly the same. Probably a lot of it is just superstition, but round here at least there does appear to be a very persistent grounding in fact. Anyone who comes face to face with the Shucca is said to die on the spot."

"Funnily enough, old Winston Churchill always used to refer to his fits of depression as 'being visited by my black dog'. And did you know that after the First World War he used to come up here from London for weekends and stay at Kingsmere Lodge on the far side of the Hope. I have always wondered..."

He drifted away for a moment, leaving Thorneycroft to consider all that he had been told. There were the makings of a fantastic story here. All he had to do was entwine the different threads... and Winston Churchill himself. What a story this would be.

Lost in his thoughts for a moment, he didn't realise that the vicar had resumed his commentary.

"...searching for its creator. If it can find and kill the man who spawned it before he finds an end to his misery then it can take on an existence of its own, independent of the dark emotions that were its unnatural birth. Legend has it that once free of its master, it will join the wild hunt and run free across heath and marsh for evermore. It seems to me that judging by the number of times the village is reputed to have been visited by the Shucca, that wild hunt must be quite a size by now."

Travers indicated towards a carving, a heraldic symbol placed high up on the wall of the church.
"There, there you go. That is what I wanted to show you."

The carving, which for all its obvious age was still clearly visible, depicted what appeared to be a bishop in full vestments. In one hand he held a mitre whilst in the other he carried a horn. Behind him stood a stag with a crucifix suspended between its antlers whilst at his feet their lay a large hound.

"Who is it?"

"Why, that's St Hubert, the man who gave his name to this very church. Strange isn't it. When I first came here I wondered about the choice of saint for the dedication of this church. St Hubert of Liege. From Germany, or rather from whatever it was called back in the seventh century. He was converted to Christianity while out hunting deer I believe. Always been associated with hunting and particularly with hounds."

He gave Thorneycroft a meaningful look before continuing.

"Throughout the Middle Ages he was often invoked as a means of dealing with misbehaving dogs or hunting hounds. Now why do you suppose that some obscure German saint would have been chosen as the patron of this little village church?"

"They knew? They chose the saint specifically because they were already being plagued by this hound?"

"Possibly, possibly. Or perhaps it is the very presence of this church and its unusual dedication that has something to do with the existence of these unnatural hounds. At least that was what I thought when I first came here and found out about the Shucca and St Hubert."

He moved back into the centre of the church, leaving his companion to study the carving.

"But after reading what old Tomkins had written and doing a bit of research myself, I realised that the hounds have probably been terrorising this corner of the county since long before the church was here. Have you ever noticed, for example, that the church is set within a perfectly circular enclosure, or that the tower is built on the remains of an earlier mound?"

He pointed down the aisle to the far end of the church, where the walls of the tower joined with those of the nave.

"There, you see? You can see where the tower has subsided slightly because of the unstable ground of the mound below and has pulled away from rest of the church. It cost us a fortune about ten years ago, getting it all underpinned to make sure the whole thing didn't fall down. We had the archaeologists in at the same time. They were interested in the mound, you see. They said it dated to the Bronze Age, I believe. They found a whole series of pits around the edge of the enclosure and do you know what was in those pits?"

Thorneycroft had followed the vicar back towards the small room where the kettle was merrily boiling away. He shook his head in answer to the reverend's question.

"Bones. Piles and piles of dog bones. The whole church was surrounded by pits full of dog bones, all dating back nearly four thousand years."

He arched his eyebrows.

"Sort of answers the question of which was here first, doesn't it?"

Thorneycroft had thought he intended returning to the small room where the books lay upon the table awaiting their attention. But as the vicar reached the door a small bell could be heard tinkling somewhere outside. He stopped abruptly and turned back towards the alter, closing his eyes for a moment and muttering a few words before turning to face the young writer.

"It is a shame we do not have more time to discuss this."

He gently began to hustle Thorneycroft back into the aisle, continuing his explanation even as he guided his charge down towards the large wooden door under the tower at the opposite end of the church.

"Plenty has been written about this but little of it has really got to the crux of the story. What the books do not tell you is that this church was indeed built and dedicated for a specific purpose."

"I understand that, as a place of sanctuary, to keep the dog at bay. That is obvious."

"No, no, I am afraid you misunderstand. The villagers here long ago learnt that nothing can stop the hound once it has been created. It will continue to seek out its master, its maker and will not rest until it has done so. The only question is how many innocent lives will be lost before it completes its quest. So far this week already, three unfortunate souls have been taken. Three people who were unlucky enough to encounter the beast while it hunted another."

Thorneycroft stopped dead in his tracks.

"What? What do you mean? Do you mean Mrs Marshall? But she had a heart attack. And the teacher? I mean, people die all the time. You can't blame every death in the village on some mysterious hellhound. It is probably just some big dog on the prowl. Are you telling me you honestly believe that people are dying in the village because of this... this Shucca?"

The vicar regarded him sadly for a moment.

"This is not the first time we have faced this dilemma. Nor, I am afraid is it likely to be the last. But we deal with it in the best way we can and hope that the Lord will forgive us when we go before him."

Reverend Travers began to back away down the aisle towards the altar, leaving Thorneycroft stood beneath the tower just inside the church door.

"It's a matter of self-preservation you see. If we help the hound by locating the man responsible for its creation, by making sure that the beast finishes its hunt as quickly as possible then we can bring the whole thing to an end before anyone else is marked. That is the true purpose of this church. That is the real reason for its unusual dedication to Saint Hubert of Liege. I would speculate that was the purpose of the pagan mound on this site even before Christianity arrived. Who knows how long this beast, or its forebears, have hunted across the Hope. All we know is that when the beast is released, we will do everything we can to make its manifestation as short as possible. Which is, unfortunately, rather bad news for you."

The confusion that the young man felt turned quickly to fear, as he heard the scrape of the door as it swung back across the uneven, stone flagged floor. Turning sharply to see who was there, he saw that the door was being dragged open by a rope attached to the large iron ring that served as a handle. The rope ran away to the right through a hole in the church wall and was obviously being operated by someone hidden outside.

As the door swung back to its full extent, Thorneycroft looked out into the dank, dimly lit graveyard. He already knew what he expected to see and there, just inside the lytch gate, stood the great dark mass of muscle, bone and sinew, no figment of his imagination, no ghostly apparition, the Shucca in all its terrible, terrifying reality.

The writer began to back slowly away down the aisle towards the altar, his heart pounding so hard he thought it must surely burst, his mind reeling as he tried, and failed, to understand what was happening, what had led him to this place and to the fate he saw before him. Of the vicar there was no sign. He was alone with the monstrous hound, as it padded slowly up the gravel path towards the door and stood, silent, on the threshold of the church. Now at last he could see it clearly.

The sleek, satin black pelt rippled ominously as the creature moved through the door and into the church, filling the space beneath the tower, so huge was its body. Wide, hunched shoulders supported a neck as thick the trunk of a tree up which ran great, cord like tendons, tensing and straining as the beast turned his head back and forth, searching the church for any other signs of life.

The temperature in the church dropped rapidly as the Shucca advanced. Every breath from its vast cavernous mouth was exhaled in a thick moist cloud, shrouding its head. But, even with the rest of its visage masked by that misty breath, one feature remained horrifyingly clear. Like black pits filled with crushed rubies, the unnatural eyes drilled through the haze and looked deep into Thorneycroft's soul. He felt a constriction in his chest, his breath became ragged and he staggered back, up a step, until he could go no further, his retreat blocked by the large stone altar. It seemed that, like so many others before him, he was to fall victim to this supernatural hound of hell.

And yet, even as the beast made its final approach and his whole world darkened in the shadows cast by those luminescent blood red eyes, the great Shucca hesitated. In that moment, when all seemed lost, a strange sense developed in the writer's mind. However much he might analyse it in later years he could not for the life of him fathom what happened in those few seconds but quite suddenly, even as he prepared himself for death, he realised that the beast could do him no harm. In the two days since he had first seen the hound as it prowled along the track behind his house, his overwhelming feeling of despair had quite simply evaporated. The simple knowledge of this unnatural hound had been sufficient to reinvigorate him, to drive out the foul black humour that had infected him for so long. And in so doing he had removed the very thing that had called forth the beast in the first place. Its very existence had depended upon his depression and now that that had dissipated, he knew that the Shucca had lost all power over him.

Even as he grasped at these thoughts, the beast hesitated, slunk back, its unholy eyes beginning to fade, to lose their diamond lustre. The monster seemed to shrink, it began to cower, to whine in a manner most unbecoming of a creature of the netherworld. As Thorneycroft took a step forward, the fiendish hound slumped back onto its haunches and threw back its head to emit a mournful, soul wrenching howl. It took the breath from the writer's lungs and drove iron nails through his skull, sending him reeling back, tripping over the step and sprawling at the foot of the altar.

And as the howl ended and the terrible echoes faded away into the furthest recesses of the church, so too did the Shucca slowly fade from view, melting into the air as if it had never existed.

We Can See You

How would we recognise a ghost if we came face to face with one? Have you passed a ghost in the street and never known its true nature? The traditional image of a semi-transparent apparition clad in period costume drifting along a midnight corridor might satisfy most people's preconceptions but what about the ghost of the man who died yesterday? Or a year ago? Or even fifty years ago? Would they look that different to you or I in dress or mannerisms?

Given the way in which our society has become ever more insular and people hardly exchange eye contact let alone greetings when they pass in the street these days, how do you know that those people who pass you by are living, breathing mortals and not simply the shadows of a former life now lost forever? Perhaps the world is filled with ghosts in plain view and we simply don't realise it.

And perhaps that is just as well.

We Can See You

Try as he might, Don Hodgekiss had never managed to stop the door to the CCTV control room squealing as it opened and closed. After endless complaints to Maintenance and a succession of visits from coveralled, whistling engineers – none of whom had managed to get to the root of the problem – he had finally given up on anyone else finding a solution and had taken it upon himself to end what he referred to as "that infernal racket". Truth be told, the squeaking was not that loud and no one else amongst the surveillance and security team had ever really been bothered by it. But to Don it was an intolerable noise that clawed at his ears like hard chalk on a blackboard, and every time someone entered or left the room a shudder went down his spine as the door screeched open and then squealed shut again. He went so far, one quiet night, as to remove the whole door and try to grease the hinges. But his technical skills did not extend to being able to re-hang it single-handedly, and his efforts earned him more than a few angry words from the Maintenance Department and an official warning letter from Human Resources. Still, once properly replaced, the door continued to squeal away merrily, as if mocking all his efforts to silence it.

Mind you, since the squeaking door amounted to the sum of all Don's problems, most people would say that he had very few cares in the world and little reason for complaint. The same probably could not be said for his colleagues. For them, the biggest fly in their ointment and the only really annoying noise in the centre was Don himself.

It was a Saturday afternoon in late spring. Shoppers drifted along Low Gate or slipped contentedly in and out of the more genteel, exclusive boutiques on Church Street. The cafés around the old market square were filled to overflowing and from the public houses came the alternate cheers and groans as football hopes were raised and dashed in the last game of the season. In the passages of the monolithic, brick built precinct - a planners dream and a shopper's nightmare, which had been constructed over the ancient winding streets behind the market - youths lolled like gibbons, taunting each other and swearing at the frightened old ladies who wheeled their trolleys across the broken, treacherous paving stones en route to the relative safety of the bus station.

The local police were out in force which, in these days of cut backs and paperwork, meant there were three officers to cover the whole of Aldwark town centre and the riverside hostelries. With tempers running high as fanatical supporters watched their teams relegated on the pub screens and with the local low lives out in force to strip the fashion shops of anything small enough to slip into a bra or pocket, it was just this sort of situation that the council control centre and its mass of close circuit cameras had been designed for.

Don loved Saturday afternoons. Whilst his colleagues might prefer the peace and quiet of the graveyard shift or the routine work of a weekday afternoon, for Don Saturdays were something special. He would gladly volunteer to work every Friday night and Saturday because it was only then, when the town was bustling busy and the police were stretched to the limit, that he felt he was really doing something worthwhile – catching the scrotes who made life a misery for decent men and women going about their lawful business.

In this way, Don was different from the other surveillance operators. For most of them this was a job – a relatively easy workday, a pay-cheque at the end of the week and, eventually, the chance of promotion or even better, being headhunted by one of the private security firms who acted as consultants to the local council. For a few it was something to be endured – the means to an end which meant they would put up with the hours of boring observation and routine paperwork so that they had the money in their pockets to allow them to go out at the weekend and make drunken fools of themselves in front of the very same cameras they had spent all week ignoring.

But for Don this was a mission – a crusade even. He hated what he saw in those cameras day in, day out. For him it was just one more sign of the imminent collapse of society and the destruction of everything he held to be of value – good manners, self-discipline and basic common courtesy. The country was going to the dogs and he was recording every minute of it on tape.

In this there was much about Don to be admired. Although not an old man, his view of the world was of an earlier generation; one that still held to the proper way of doing things. Many of his colleagues even had some small, grudging respect for him and his unwavering stand against the decadence of modern society – if only he wouldn't rattle on about it all the bloody time!

Don knew all the civil liberties arguments about CCTV and their ever-growing intrusion into the lives of the public. In spite of his job he even agreed with most of them. The population were being spied upon by an overzealous and illiberal government. They were being driven wholesale into a surveillance society by a nanny state. Anyone with half a brain could see that. But, in the final analysis, in spite of understanding and agreeing with the civil libertarians on almost every major philosophical objection, when it came to real world, he simply didn't care.

The reason was simple.

He was the one doing the spying, not the one being spied upon.

And if you knew where the cameras were placed and how they worked, what their limitations were and how they could be avoided by someone with just a little inside knowledge, then, as he liked to expound to his colleagues, the simple answer to the old chestnut "Quis custodiet ipsos custodes?" was "neminis".

As long as, that is, like Don, you had received a classical education. Otherwise, as with so much else that poured forth from his mouth, it was just so much gibberish.

So it was that, in his own mind at least, Don found himself at the forefront of a battle to win back civilisation from the beast of modern society; to drive the thugs and thieves, the chavs and ladettes, the unemployed and unemployable from the streets and return the country to its days of mythical former glory. To achieve this aim he would use any tool, any means at his disposal. He saw himself as the eyes and perhaps - if that new budget request for upgraded cameras with microphones went through -even the ears of the men and women keeping the streets safe for decent, hard working, tax paying folk.

On this particular Saturday afternoon Don was in the hot seat. With two of his colleagues – both of whom had one lazy eye on the cameras and the other on the football drama being played out on the small TV in the corner of the office - he was helping the police to protect both the health and the wealth of the traders and shoppers in the bustling town centre. As always, he reflected that the town did not seem quite as bustling as he remembered from a decade ago. He put this down to a combination of the stupid council policies which built over car parks and charged an extortionate amount for the few spaces that remained, and the general economic climate after so many years of mismanagement by the hated government. Well hated by Don anyway.

Whatever the causes, the shop keepers were complaining of falling sales, tighter margins and the prospect of selling up and moving their businesses to one of the bigger towns or cities where the local politicians had more thought for the people who brought in the wealth and paid the taxes. Don knew they would always moan about something and doubted that many of them would act on their threats, but he had to admit that they had a point. What he saw through his cameras every day certainly backed up the shopkeepers' complaints. What was strange was that the councillors didn't seem to see it. Every week they would write in the local paper defending their decisions and claiming that the town was bustling busy with people and that if they weren't spending then that was clearly the fault of the shopkeepers, not their elected representatives.

It was a long time since Don had ventured into town when the shops were open. He tended to do his shopping at the local supermarket, following his wife round dutifully whilst she filled the trolley with the same uninspiring foods from the same uninspiring list every Friday afternoon. Any special purchases he left to his spouse, content to let her waste her time wandering round the shops and playing the lottery that was the local bus service. As a result, the only impression he had of the town was the one he gained via his cameras and, if they were anything to go by, then the shoppers did indeed seem to be thin on the ground these days.

Don's musings were interrupted by a squawking, barely audible message on the radio that sat on the desk in front of him. Many of the local shopkeepers had paid into a system which allowed them to communicate instantly both with each other and with the CCTV centre. They used the radios to share up to the minute information on the various suspicious characters who drifted in and out of their premises or who loitered in the street outside – perhaps looking for an opportunity, when an assistant's back was turned, to dash into a shop and whip something off a shelf without being noticed. Such was the nature of shop keeping in modern Britain.

This particular squawk was from Mrs Hayman at the off licence. She had spotted a couple of 'notorious' youths skulking in a doorway opposite her shop, obviously, to her mind at least, up to no good and planning an afternoon's thievery and thuggery. Thus, the well-practiced system swung into operation. A general warning about known undesirables as they were first spotted alerted both the shopkeepers and the CCTV centre to their presence. A description was circulated which emphasised hooded jackets, sneakers and baseball caps – obvious outward expressions of innate criminality. From that moment on, for the rest of the afternoon until they deigned to leave the town centre, their every move would be traced via a series of cameras and personal sightings and would be reported to the network. This would ensure that, should they undertake the slightest act of delinquency, real or imagined, they would be swooped upon in an instant and subjected to the full force of the law – or if, as it so often did, that failed to materialise, then the cameras could suffer a short and unexplained technical fault whilst a suitable amount of vigilante vengeance was exacted.

Don made a quick note of the description on his notepad in tight, neat handwriting and started rotating the cameras on Staines Gate to locate his targets. He glanced over at his two colleagues to see if they were taking any interest in the alert, but they were now lost in the last few minutes of the big match on the small screen. Totally oblivious to the job at hand, they would be of little use until the final whistle had blown – and in Don's opinion not much better after that either. He sighed and shook his head with resignation. Once again it was left to him alone to protect decent people like Mrs Hayman from the degenerates who plagued their town.

And there they were, just as she had described. Hoods pulled up over caps whose brims were dragged down low over shrouded faces. Their visages further masked by the haze of smoke from cigarettes hanging from slack bottom lips. One hand shoved deep into tracksuit pockets whilst the other grasped a mobile phone that would only be removed by surgery or death. Evolution and street fashion had long removed any trace of necks and their heads were slumped so far forward that the tops of their ears were the same level as the tops of their shoulders. They walked with a shuffling, lurching gait that was half orangutan, half zombie. They were the next stage in human evolution and it was clearly to be a retrograde step.

Right now the two youths – it was impossible to tell whether they were male or female – were standing in the doorway of the newsagents, deep in conversation – although as far as Don was concerned, the use of either the word 'deep' or 'conversation' when describing the monosyllabic language of these creatures was seriously misleading. He envisaged them exchanging a series of inarticulate grunts which would quickly degenerate into physical violence if they attempted to express any concept higher than eat, drink, smoke or steal. Every minute or so they would glance up at the opaque glass dome which housed the CCTV camera, clearly aware that they might be under observation and uncomfortable with the idea that their, undoubtedly criminal, activities were being recorded.

"Yes, you little sods," Don muttered under his breath, "I can see you."

It had become something of a mantra over the years. "You can't escape me. Wherever you go, I can see you."

As the camera network had spread throughout the town there had become fewer and fewer main thoroughfares that were beyond Don's vision. But the many passageways and snickleways that ran between the streets, remnants of the network of old covered paths and passages that had linked the yards and alleys of the medieval town, were still out of sight of the CCTV system. The skill of an operator lay in knowing where each passage led when it left a street. If a suspect ducked away into the hidden maze of snickleways that crisscrossed the town, where was he most likely to reappear? It was this skill in predicting the movements of the targets through the back alleys which marked out a good operator. And Don wasn't just good, he was great.

As he watched, the two youths finished their dubious business and set off down the street towards the town centre. Stalking down Town Gate and into the market square, hands buried deep in their pockets and heads down, seemingly oblivious to crowds around them, they barged their way through shoppers laden with bags, growling insults and threats at anyone who dared to comment on their uncouth behaviour. Passing right across the market square and on down Steadman Gate, they washed up on the doorstep of the tiny newsagents and off licence on the corner of Castle Boulevard. Their whole journey of perhaps 500 yards had been tracked on no less than 6 cameras, and three separate shops had reported their progress on the radio network. Don knew that these two were old hands at this game and would have realised that their every move had been followed since they first loped into town. Surely they would have to be fools to try anything under those circumstances.

Of course one should never underestimate just how many fools there are in the world; particularly young, proud fools too stupid to realise the depths of their own ignorance. In spite of the presence of cameras, which had proved their downfall more than once in the recent past, the two hooded youths swung into action, following a well-rehearsed and depressingly familiar plan.

It took less than a minute to execute the crime and, whilst he may not have had a camera inside the shop, Don knew only too well what the two delinquents were doing whilst out of his sight.

For all their air of menace as they stalked through the streets, they would not use force to achieve their ends.

Rather they would show a cunning that belied their troglodyte appearance. They had picked their target well; the owner of the shop, a small, balding, aged man whose skin had yellowed after half a century of exposure to unceasing cigarette smoke, was renowned for his miserliness and avarice. He refused to employ an assistant because he could not bring himself to pay a half way decent wage. As a result, he alone would man the premises from seven in the morning to six at night, shutting briefly whenever he had to leave his counter to pop through to the cramped damp rooms in which he lived at the back of the decaying Victorian corner terrace. Nor would he be on the local shop radio network as he was unwilling to pay the few pounds a month it cost to contribute to the maintenance of the system.

Though well aware of what these two youths probably intended and in spite of having been fooled and robbed on numerous occasions in the past, they well knew that, given the right lure of a big enough sale, the shopkeeper could be persuaded to turn his back upon his till for a few moments in order to clamber up a small set of steps to retrieve a carton of cigarettes or a bottle of vodka from the upper reaches of his shelves. To ease his suspicion, the young thieves did not enter the shop together but instead had one enter first, to distract the old man, whilst the other followed half a minute later, checked that the keeper's back was turned, and reached over the counter to remove whatever was lying in the open till.

If they got it right, then they could be out of the shop and off up the street before the owner had time to clamber down from his steps. If they got it right.

Of course in crime, as in war, no plan survives first contact with the enemy. Don would never know what exactly transpired out of sight of his camera, but it was clear from the speed and fear with which the two, would-be thieves left the shop, that things had not gone well for them in their illegal endeavour. Stumbling one over the other in their haste to escape, they barrelled out onto the street and accelerated away, back towards the centre of town, hoping to reach the relative safety of the bustling market square where they could lose any pursuit amongst the crowds of shoppers. But Don had not simply been idly sitting, watching developments. As soon as it was clear which unfortunate shopkeeper was the target of the thieves, he had alerted the meagre police presence and, with the experience born of years of watching, had directed the only two available officers to the route he rightly guessed would be that most likely to be taken by the youths in their attempts to escape.

As the irate shopkeeper appeared at the door of his shop carrying what appeared to be a broom handle with a carving knife tied to the end, the first of the youths, head down, not realising he was already caught, careered into the waiting arms of the two officers. With an aplomb that impressed Don, watching through his cameras, one policeman pirouetted the captive into the embrace of his fellow officer and darted off in pursuit of the second thief.

The boy – his hood now thrown off his head to reveal he was indeed a male – darted across the road, skipping over the bonnet of a parked car and plunged into through a narrow archway into one of the hidden alleys. The lawman was only moments behind him.

For a few brief minutes they were lost from the view of the cameras. But Don was unperturbed. The back alley, down which the youth and his pursuit had disappeared, had only one exit – on the corner of the main market square just opposite the church – and the watcher was already realigning the cameras on the front of the town hall to give him a clear view of the exit. He was in time to see the thief ricochet out of the alleyway, swerve around an old man and dart across the square and back down yet another alleyway on the far side of a café.

It was only a matter of a few dozen yards but it was far enough that, before he had reached the shadows of the snickleway, the policeman had emerged from the first alley and should clearly have had his quarry in his sights.

Then, unbelievably, the pursuer hesitated.

"Which way?" He gasped into his radio as he pulled up outside the café, almost scattering the arrangement of small tables and chairs across the pavement.

"What do you mean which way?" Don could not hide the incredulity from his voice. "He was there right in front of you. How could you have missed him? Are you blind or something?"

The reply was curt. "How the bloody hell am I supposed to see him in all these people. Now which way did he go?"

Don was becoming more confused by the second. Apart from the old man and a couple sat drinking coffee at one of the tables, the area between the policeman and the alleyway he should have seen the boy enter was completely empty. There was no way that the officer could have failed to see where the boy went and with each passing second as he stood gazing about him there was less chance he would ever catch up with the thief. Don quickly realised that the hesitation had been fatal and that their quarry was probably already safely lost in the maze of alleys beyond the church.

"What do you mean 'all these people'? He was right there in front of you. Use your eyes man. Get after him."

The young policeman – not for the first time, Don wondered why it was that they all looked like they should be wearing a boy scout rather than a police uniform – was stood on the pavement staring up at the camera with a look of confusion and anger painted across his face. It was clear from the strain in his voice as he spoke curtly into the radio that he was of the opinion that Don was either deluded or trying to make a fool out of him.

"What the hell are you talking about? How on earth am I supposed to see him through a street full of people, you old fool? I asked you a simple question. Which way did he go? It's alright for you with your cameras up on those poles, but down here at street level I can't see a bloody thing through these crowds."

"Don't you use that tone with me mate." Don was getting angry himself now and as he raised his voice his two companions turned away from the game on the television to see what all the commotion was about. "Copper or no copper, you ought to get your eyes tested. You're seeing things."

The policeman looked about him in disbelief as if searching for someone to back up his story and decisively prove the man on the other end of the camera wrong. He had dropped the radio microphone that was pinned to his lapel and, even though he could no longer be heard in the control room, it was clear he was muttering some very un-professional phrases, something that Don found especially disturbing in figures of authority.

Don was feeling just as frustrated as the policeman. The second thief should have been an easy catch but now, as he scanned the cameras that watched almost every major street in the centre, he could see no sign of the youth. Their quarry had gone to ground and, if he had any sense, he would stay there until things had quietened down and he could slip quietly away back to his sink estate on the fringes of the town, free to try his hand another day at stealing the hard-won takings of honest shopkeepers.

He slammed his radio down on the desk in disgust and swung around, out of his chair to stalk across the room to the coffee machine leaving the policeman with his imaginary crowds and the frustration of his failed pursuit.

Whilst annoyed by the events of that May Saturday afternoon, Don was not particularly disturbed by what had unfolded. All it really did was reinforce his prejudices: All youths were little scumbags just waiting to steal the false teeth out of an old lady's mouth, the police were worse than useless and he needed more cameras to make sure there was nowhere the undesirables could hide from his ever watchful gaze. If that had been the sum total of the fallout from the mini-debacle then he would quickly have forgotten it.

But it seemed that there were those who would not let him forget. It seemed the young policeman had friends who were willing and able to take advantage of what they perceived as a failing by Don and make use of the incident to undermine his position. At least that was how he interpreted the events of the weeks that followed.

On the following Thursday he found himself in an almost identical conversation with another officer.

"She's there, man, about 40 yards ahead of you on the corner by the bank. She must be in plain view. Are you blind or something?"

"There are too many people here. What did she look like again? Where is she standing?"

And on the Friday night by the taxi rank outside the nightclub.

"Look, it's the two lads on the left. They are the ones who started the fight."

"Which ones do you mean? There are about twenty of them here. You have to be more specific."

In the three weeks or so that following the first incident there were no less than a dozen occasions in which Don was left thinking something was seriously wrong with either his cameras, his eyes, or the mental state of the officers of the Aldwark police force. Nor was it only the uniforms who seemed to be infected by the idiocy. By the end of the second week some of the shopkeepers were also making him think that they had lost their minds. He wondered why he had never noticed it before. Conversations over the radio net about customers who seemed to be invisible to his cameras, complaints about people loitering outside shops when there was clearly no one in sight. It was as if everyone were conspiring to make him doubt the evidence of his own eyes. He had long since stopped challenging their accounts for fear of exposing himself to even more ridicule. If it carried on like this then he couldn't see how he could continue in his job. He was becoming a laughing stock.

Something would have to be done.

There was still little conviction in Don's mind that anything was really amiss with either his cameras or his own eyesight. He had yet to be convinced that this was anything more than an elaborate and extremely ill-considered wind-up. But truth be told, the first seeds of doubt had been sown. Knowing, as he did, how these things could fester and grow if not nipped in the bud good and early, he resolved to contrive a small test to reassure himself that all was as it should be and that it really was just a case of mischievous officers and shopkeepers letting a practical joke run just that bit too far. If and when he had determined that was the case, Don had decided to adopt an air of dignified silence and ignore any further attempts to make him appear foolish.

He was a methodical man who didn't rush into things without careful consideration; and so he considered; carefully. The best starting point would be to assume, just for a moment, that the officers were not pulling a fast one, that somehow the cameras were indeed failing to record people who were standing right there in front of them. However ridiculous this idea might appear, it was the only alternative – apart from his favoured explanation of an elaborate practical joke – of which he could conceive. Don knew and had often quoted Holmes' famous maxim;

"When you have eliminated the impossible, whatever remains, however improbable, must be the truth."

This seemed like a perfect example of just such a situation. If the policemen were not lying – although he still considered this the most likely scenario – then there must be something happening to the cameras to prevent him seeing whoever was standing in the street, clearly in plain view of those actually on the scene.

His first task would be to verify that there was indeed something amiss. Since he had strong doubts about the veracity of the police – God, that it should come to the point that he now even doubted the one group of people he had believed absolutely trustworthy – the only evidence he would now believe was that provided by his own eyes, unfiltered by cameras, cables and monitors.

It seemed a simple enough task. He chose a Saturday afternoon again since that had been the day when the first incident had occurred. As always seemed to be the case these days, the town looked relatively quiet on his monitors whilst the police were reporting it just as busy as ever and the shop keepers moaned openly on the radios – in clear violation of the accepted procedures – that for all the people on the streets, no one seemed to be coming in to spend much money. It appeared that this was a perfect opportunity to test once and for all whether there was any foundation to his doubts.

It was a no great problem to find an excuse to slip out for twenty minutes leaving the other operators to cover for him. The reason given was that he needed to get a present for his wife for their anniversary. Strictly speaking that was true. What his colleagues didn't need to know was that Don never bought the presents for his wife. He was more than happy to pay for them and never begrudged any money spent on her, it was just that he never actually bought them himself. He had long ago learnt that his judgement in almost every aspect of his wife's taste and preferences was seriously defective and that the best he could hope for was a wan smile and a 'oh that's nice dear, thank you'. At worst he would make some dreadful faux pas such as buying clothes which were miles too big or too small and as a consequence would spend days or even weeks in the proverbial doghouse. So for an easy life and a clear conscience he had acquiesced when, a number of years earlier, his wife had suggested that perhaps she would pick the presents and, to maintain the illusion that they had originated with him, Don, who was a dab hand with paper and tape, would wrap them and present them to her as and when necessary. An arrangement which suited them both very well

So it was that, just after lunch, Don slipped out of the council offices and off up the hill towards the market square. According to his monitors there were perhaps a few score of people passing back and forth across the cobbled market place and, as he turned off Orchard Gate and strode through the park behind the church, the lack of picnickers gave him cause to believe that he would find the town to be just as quiet as it had appeared from the control room.

He rounded the corner of the church and stopped, dead in his tracks, mouth agape as he stared across the street, through the narrow archway that led to the square.

The place was heaving.

It was early that same evening and Don was back at his desk, staring at the bank of screens arrayed before him. But, for perhaps the first time in his career, he was seeing nothing of the mundane events that unfolded on the monitors.

He had returned to the market square three more times that day. Each time he had spent a few moments watching in disbelief as people hustled and bustled through the town, in and out of shops, strolling, running, sitting and standing. Going about their everyday lives, oblivious to the turmoil they were causing in the mind of one man. Then, still not believing the evidence of his own eyes, he would rush back to the control room and stare at the same square, the same streets and shops, through his cameras. And there he would see a scene utterly different to the one he had just left a few minutes earlier. Try as he might he could find no logical way to reconcile the two scenes. The pictures recorded and transmitted by his cameras showed perhaps only a quarter of the people he had seen wandering through the town square. The rest, many hundreds of men, women and children, were seemingly invisible to modern technology. To all intents and purposes they simply weren't there.

Now he knew why it was the policemen – and he really wasn't looking forward to having to apologise to them for having doubted their word – had claimed to be unsighted by crowds of people he could not see. To the naked eye the whole town seemed to be filled with... with what? Ghosts? It was a word that sprang readily to mind but it was also one that he tried just as readily to dismiss. Whilst he could conceive of no rational explanation for what he was observing, he certainly wasn't ready to simply roll over and accept that this was because of some sort of supernatural phenomena.

That was, of course, before his fourth and final visit to the square that day. He wasn't quite sure why he had been drawn back that one last time. It was already clear that something was seriously awry with either the cameras or his mind and to keep returning to the town centre, to spend long minutes staring at the seemingly perfectly normal people passing before him, would in no way contribute to his greater understanding of this mysterious turn of events. Or so he believed.

Even though the evening was drawing on, less than a month short of mid-summer, one side of the square was still bathed in bright sunshine as the shops drew down their shutters and closed their doors on another day's mediocre trading. Although the crowds had thinned noticeably from his previous visits there were still plenty of people strolling across the square, avoiding the council workers as they dismantled the stalls and swept away the accumulated rubbish of the traditional Saturday market. There was simply nothing apparently out of the ordinary to see here – at least not to anyone who didn't carry the memory of the images from the security cameras seared into their brains.

After a fruitless twenty minutes spent watching, searching for anything that might help him unravel this mystery, Don had finally exhaled one, long held breath, stood up from his seat on the edge of the park and turned to walk back down the hill to the control centre.

And it was at that moment that he had seen it.

For a split second he hadn't been quite sure whether or not his mind had finally and irrevocably cracked. Could there be any other explanation? He hadn't seen it out of the corner of his eye. It could not, by any stretch of the imagination, have been a mistake, the result of misty eyes, bad light or any other optical illusion. He had seen it. In broad daylight and without a shadow of a doubt.

There, less than ten feet from him, a young boy chasing a runaway ball, had ran straight through a man and woman walking arm in arm. The boy hadn't run between them. He hadn't swerved around them, knocked them to one side or darted between their legs. They hadn't even appeared to notice his presence which, considering he had just passed right through their bodies, was somewhat surprising. He had simply run straight through them as if they weren't there. Neither the boy nor the couple had exhibited the slightest reaction to indicate they were aware of the existence of the other party in the apparent collision. It was as if they were inhabiting entirely separate realities.

Don had slumped down suddenly again on the bench. He had sat there, motionless, for a long, long time. How long he couldn't say for sure but by the time he had come back to his senses both the couple, the boy and most of the rest of the passing pedestrians had moved on and the market square was bereft of life but for the council workers putting the last few barrowloads of rubbish and refuse into the back of their truck. He had felt dizzy, slightly sick and feverish. The warm breeze which dusted across the park and whispered through the trees had brought little relief and it had taken all his strength to force himself up out of the seat once more and wander, dazed, punch drunk, back towards the sanctuary of his office.

And now he was back at his desk, facing those same treacherous screens which had failed him so badly, oblivious to the hushed conversations of his colleagues who had watched his comings and goings with increasing bemusement as the afternoon wore on. He had looked so unwell after his first, supposed shopping, trip that they had decided to track his progress as he bounced back and forth between the council offices and the town centre. In part, this was a voyeuristic impulse driven by the hope that they might catch a glimpse of whatever it was that had him so shaken. News of his strange behaviour that afternoon had spread beyond the control room onto the network of shopkeepers, security guards and policemen who were tied to the shopwatch system. As is the unfortunate nature of such environments, there was already a book open on the reason for his apparent distress, with the odds on favourite being that he had accidently stumbled across his wife in the arms of another man. But there was also, amongst some of the operators at least, an underlying nagging concern that perhaps there was something seriously wrong with Don. He may have been an annoying, opinionated pedant at times but, in all honesty, they wouldn't have wished any great harm to befall him.

But if they hoped for some enlightenment from their cameras then, just like Don, they were to be sorely disappointed. By the time he returned from his last trip up the hill looking, as one of his colleagues perceptively commented, 'as if he had seen a ghost', they had tired of their spying and, since he did not look to be in imminent danger of doing himself any damage, had decided it was much simpler just to huddle up by the coffee machine and create a good bit of gossip of their own instead.

Don, meanwhile, sat and stared.

He was not a man easily given to losing control, to breaking down at the first sign of adversity. His undistinguished exterior belied an inner strength of character that would have surprised many of his friends and colleagues. In the main they saw only the bluster and the constant carping and, if they had considered it at all, had long ago concluded that this was an outer expression of underlying insecurities. To quote the old saying; few of them would have wanted him to be in their trench. But, as it turned out, they were seriously underestimating the man. Whilst thoroughly shaken by the events of the day, Don was not, by any means, reduced to a quivering wreck. His blustering persona and critical temperament were rooted in a genuine ability to outthink most of his colleagues. By any subjective measure he was indeed considerably brighter than most of those around him. It was just a shame that he knew it and usually combined this knowledge with a lack of tolerance for those he considered slower and less able than himself.

So whilst it might have appeared to the rest of the control room that Don had sunk into a semi- permanent state of nervous exhaustion, once the initial shock had passed, his mind had rapidly settled itself upon the task of sifting, isolating and analysing all the available data with the aim of producing a coherent narrative to explain, once and for all, what the bloody hell was going on.

As far as he could see, the facts of the case were few and seemed pretty straightforward. There were, walking the streets of Aldwark, large numbers of people – seemingly otherwise perfectly normal people – who refused – if that was the right word to use as it assumed an active intent – who failed rather, to appear on the security cameras. Furthermore it seemed, from his observation of the collision between the boy and the young couple, that at least some of these people were rather less than corporeal in the sense that most folk understood that term. Not to put too polite a label on them, they were phantoms.

The questions rattled noisily around his mind like bone dice in a tin cup. How long this had been going on was unknown. How many of the people one passed in the street every day were similarly spectral in origin? Were they the shades of sadly departed? Were they the projection of some sort of electromagnetic interference, some recording of past events with no more foundation in reality than a television picture? Were they conscious of their existence, of their surroundings, of their true nature? Were they dangerous?

He was mildly surprised to find it had taken him so long to get to that last question. It was not something that had registered in his thoughts until that moment and he realised that he had so far assumed, subconsciously at least, that these phantoms were no threat to himself or anyone else. If it were indeed the case that they had been walking the streets of Aldwark for many years, then they certainly seemed to have done so without causing either harm or even alarm to any of the liv... the living? Was he already making that distinction between the electronically visible and the invisible?

No matter. Whatever their true nature, his first task had to be to find a way to observe and record these apparitions on his screens. Only then could he start to unravel their true nature.

This was a technical problem – one that needed some technical assistance to resolve it. And Don knew just the person to turn to.

As has already been intimated, Don Hodgekiss was not actually a bad person and for all the people who would gladly have strangled the man with his own microphone cord, there were just as many – admittedly those who did not have to deal with him on a daily basis in an enclosed space – who considered him a valuable friend, a man who could be trusted and relied upon and someone who could be turned to in times of trouble.

Amongst this small cadre of loyal admirers was Don's nephew Andy. Now a fine, dependable young man in his early twenties, Andy owed his education and job – indeed his whole adult life – to Don. The uncle had seen his nephew going off the rails as a youth of seventeen. He had shown a subtlety and insight which belied his cantankerous reputation, as he drew the boy carefully away from a life of petty street crime and drugs, providing both the money and the guidance to set him on the road to a successful career and a settled family life. As a consequence, Andy's attitude to his uncle was about as close as either would ever comfortably be to hero worship.

After ensuring he obtained a useful qualification at the town college, Don had pulled a few strings to get his nephew an apprenticeship in the technical department at the Local Council. And now, five years later, it was Andy who was responsible for the maintenance and repair of the cameras that provided Don and his fellow operators with their bird's eye view of Aldwark.

In the years since he started at the council, Andy had gained a well-deserved reputation as a technical whizz kid. Again this was something he owed, at least in part, to his uncle who had, himself, spent many happy days in his youth messing around with electronics, taking apart the radio or television – much to the anger and frustration of his parents – and successfully rebuilding them again afterwards – much to their relief.

It was that natural technical ability of both uncle and nephew that Don now wished to utilise to solve the problem of the unseen bystanders. His plan was simple. Whilst it was clear that, for whatever reason, the apparitions did not appear on the cameras, it was equally clear that they did appear to the naked eye. Whether or not they were ghosts – and in spite of all the evidence to the contrary, Don was still stubbornly resisting finally accepting such a proposition – they had to obey the basic laws of physics. He hoped.

So it had to be a simple matter of either wavelengths or transmission. Obviously there must be some difference between the way in which the camera and the eye were receiving the physical data, or between the way in which the data was being transmitted to the screen and the brain. To Don, it was simply a case of finding out where the differences lay and adapting the cameras or the transmission system to correct for their inability to 'see' the people.

Over the next few weeks, Don's colleagues saw something of a transformation in his nature. He had always been one of the most conscientious of the operators but now he was a positive demon; arriving early for shift, leaving late and, most remarkably perhaps, while he was at his console, allowing whole hours to pass without a complaint, a comment or even a mild grumble. To be sure he still found time once in a while to complain about the squeaking door but even then it seemed his heart was not really in it, that he was just going through the motions of moaning because it was somehow expected of him, that to surrender that last cantankerous characteristic would be to signal the end of civilisation as we know it.

The most common phrase to pass his lips now was the one he had made his own as he tracked the criminals and trouble makers, the muggers, pickpockets and vandals as they pursued their nefarious occupations. More so than ever before it became his mantra, hissed under his breath or laughed out loud as he watched the vain attempts of his prey to escape the justice served by his cameras;

"I can see you."

And when the other operators heard that whispered declaration they knew that someone on the other end of one of those cameras was about to have a very, very bad day.

At the same time, Don's attitude to the people he was spying upon also changed in a subtle but significant manner. Many of them may have been the low lives he had previously detested – actually he still detested them, but he did so in a rather more paternalistic manner – but at least they were undoubtedly human. They appeared on his cameras, they had life, consciousness, independent thought. Well, some of them anyway. Maybe.

But the point was that they were clearly and visibly real. He knew that because he could see them on his screens. What worried him now were not the people he could see. It was the ones he could not. The ones he knew were there, filling the streets, going about their existences unseen by his cameras.

What bothered him, what angered him far more than the acts of criminality he watched and recorded day after day, what was slowly eating away at him and driving an ever-growing paranoia, was the certain knowledge that there were other beings, other 'people' walking those same streets to whom he was utterly blind. That was a situation he could not allow to continue. That was the problem to which, more and more, he turned his attention.

He had to be cautious in his approach to the project. Unlike most other professions where one often found oneself holding the fort alone, in this case Don was rarely, if ever, alone in the control room when on shift. Nor could he simply stay behind after work in order to take advantage of the absence of his colleagues. By its very nature, the CCTV control room had to work twenty-four hours a day and was never left unmanned. If Don were not actually on shift, then at least one of his fellow operators would be present in his place. This, combined with the sensitive security nature of the work, meant that the opportunities for meddling with the system and following private projects, even if for the most honourable of reasons, were severely curtailed.

In spite of these obstacles, over the next few weeks Don managed to run a whole series of tests and adjustments to the system in an attempt to isolate how exactly the shades managed to walk the streets unseen. In this he relied greatly on the advice and covert assistance of his nephew, to whom he had explained only the barest outline of his outlandish experiences and undoubtedly extraordinary conclusions. As far as Andy was concerned, they were looking for a group of ne'er do wells who had managed to devise some sort of electronic masking device that prevented them being seen by the CCTV system. At least that what was Don told his nephew. Along with the lie that he had been secretly approached by the police and other unnamed but extremely important government agencies with a request to investigate what was happening and find some way of countering this obvious threat to the rule of law. Whilst initially sceptical, his Labrador-like trust in his uncle combined with Don's careful attention to detail in every aspect of the story, convinced Andy that this was indeed an important, perhaps even vital, operation and that it was his duty to both assist and maintain the blanket of secrecy.

And so, like latter day agents on a mission of upmost national importance to counter a great threat from powers mysterious and unknown, the two men set to work. They altered the frequency of the radio signal from the cameras, they tried imposing various filters on the signal as it arrived on the control room system. They took the images and transferred them to Andy's laptop where he attempted all manner of manipulations far beyond Don's own level of expertise, using both legitimate software and also some extremely powerful and unstable programmes downloaded from various illegal sites scattered across the internet. All to no avail. Which was, if they were being honest, much as they had expected. It had soon become clear as they began their experiments that the problem lay not with the transmission of the signal from the cameras to the monitors, but with the way in which the cameras received the raw image from the streets.

"There is no alternative, I'm afraid," admitted Andy over a cup of tea in his uncle's kitchen late one evening, after they had spent too many fruitless hours poring over frame after frame of empty streets, trying a hundred and one different programmes to try and reveal something that, quite clearly, wasn't there.

"We are going to have to go to the root of the problem. We are going to have to try filtering the picture at the cameras themselves, before the image enters the electronics. We knew that from the start really, didn't we?" He wiped his hand across his straw-stubbled scalp as he stared at the screen one more time, as if hoping that figures would somehow magically appear on those barren pavements.

"Ay, you're right." Don replied somewhat despondently, staring at his slippered feet if only to give his eyes a rest from the interminable scenes of streets almost bereft of life.

Don knew there were people on those streets, people who should have shown up on those recordings. He had stood on the corner outside the run-down newsagent's and watched them wander past him. He had been very careful about synchronising his watch with the clock on the monitor in the control room before he left, and in the hour that he had lingered by the dirt grimed window filled with newspaper headlines, old cigarette adverts and personal ads for rented rooms and lost cats, he had noted exactly when anyone moved through the field of view of the CCTV. He had chosen a time relatively late in the evening, around nine when the summer sun was already down below the roofs of the Georgian fronted shops that lined Castle Boulevard. Ostensibly this was to ensure there were not too many people about who could confuse the timings and make it difficult to later ascertain who showed up on the recordings and who did not.

But more importantly, as far as Don was concerned, it also meant that Andy – whose young family kept him occupied in the evenings – could take no part in that particular aspect of the operation. Once his nephew saw the apparently normal people – men women and especially the children – who were the subject of their investigations, there was no way Don would be able to maintain the fiction that these were all criminals pursuing such nefarious activities that they posed an imminent threat to national security.

Whilst the streets had not, for obvious reasons, been overflowing with pedestrians, and even cars had been in relatively short supply at that time in the evening, there was, never the less, a steady procession of seemingly perfectly normal people; individuals, couples and even some families, who passed under the gaze of both Don and, apparently, the CCTV cameras during the hour he spent observing and noting each passage.

By the time the church clock had been striking ten and the warm, soft dusk was firmly settling over the town, Don had counted no less than twenty-nine people walking past his vantage spot. All had seemed absolutely normal and, by the time his vigil had ended, he had been starting to have concerns as to whether or not any of them were phantoms. If they were all to appear on the raw, unprocessed video footage then it would all have been a waste of time and they would have to go through the whole process again on another evening.

But now, the following night, sat on his hard, wooden chair and staring at his slippers, Don sorely wished that they had all been real people. Of the twenty-nine individuals who had passed in front of the cameras and had been recorded in Don's notebook, only three – a lone youth loping off to the pub and a middle-aged couple probably en route to the cinema – had appeared on the footage. Of the rest there was nothing to be seen. Not a footfall, not a shadow, not a single trace of any of them. The three who had turned out to be visible had come as both a shock and a relief after all that emptiness. They had also served a useful function in proving that there was nothing otherwise wrong with the cameras and that Don had not made a mistake in transcribing the correct section of recording to disc; both possibilities that had occurred to them before the appearance of normal people on the film.

But yes, in the final analysis, Andy was absolutely right. There was nothing more they could do from the control room. If they wanted to solve this problem they would have to go out and work with the cameras themselves.

And so it was that, on yet another quiet late summer's evening, just after the sun had set and whilst Don was standing his regular shift in the control room, his nephew was out and about undertaking some essential maintenance to a number of cameras around the town. That, at least, was his official purpose. In fact, for the fourth time that month he was installing a set of new filters onto a number of the cameras, in the increasingly vain hope that they might, once and for all, reveal the men who had so far successfully managed to circumvent the whole security system.

In his heart, Andy was becoming increasingly pessimistic about their chances of solving this mystery. There was a limit to the number of times he could reasonably claim that there were problems with the cameras, and he was sure that fairly soon someone in the management was going to notice a pattern and realise that these 'failures' only ever occurred when Don was on shift, and Andy was the only person available to take the call out. One more time, he reckoned, and then that was it. One more time to push their luck and then they would finally have to admit defeat.

This particular evening the town seemed unusually quiet and Andy saw only a handful of people – all off in the distance at the far end of streets or across the other side of the square – as he completed his tasks. As he slipped down his collapsible ladder, packed it up neatly and slung it over his shoulder before picking up his tool bag from beside one of the ornate pillars that fronted the Georgian Town Hall, he felt well satisfied with the evening's work. Although it had pulled away from home for a few hours he was sure that Jenny would understand, and it wasn't as if he made a habit of it. Well, not until recently and that would soon be at an end. He would volunteer for the dishwasher filling duties to make it up to her. But in this, if in nothing else, he wanted to pull his weight and do his bit to help his uncle. Besides, there was no way Don would have been able to make the necessary adjustments to the camera himself. Not only did he lack the knowledge and experience with the sharp end of the CCTV system, but there was no way he could have made the alterations without calling attention to himself. Don was a control room operator. Andy was the instrument technician. No one would have been surprised to see him up a rickety ladder making adjustments to a dodgy camera.

He strode quickly back across the cobbled square and onto Town Gate to where he had parked his small yellow council van. The market place was deserted and almost silent but for the low hum of neon lights from the tacky, garish shop fronts which surrounded the square. Remembering that Don would need to know the work was completed before he could reset the system and start studying the pictures in the control room, he plucked his mobile from his breast pocket and hit the quick dial for his uncle. The call was answered immediately.

"Hi, uncle? Yep, it's me. Yep, all done. You should be able to restart those monitors and see if there are any changes. The colours might look a bit strange but no worse than last time."

He hesitated as he approached the corner of Town Gate and Orchard Gate, hearing a car approaching but unable to tell from which direction, as the noise of the engine echoed round the tall canyon like walls of the Georgian streets.

He continued his conversation, "Yep, just start everything up again and then give me a ring back. I am heading home so ring me there. I'll be in in about 10 minutes. Yep. Talk later. Cheers."

He pushed the red disconnect on the phone and dropped it back in his pocket. Job done. Now for home. Approaching the kerb at the corner he looked up and saw two young lads of perhaps eleven or twelve stood watching him from the other side of the road, about twenty yards down the shallow hill towards the old museum. At the same time, he saw the lights of a car approaching up the street, past the museum, past the war memorial at the back of the church. He would hardly have noticed it in the fading evening light were it not for the side lights and the over revved engine as it accelerated fast towards the town square. Probably some teenager just passed his test and out to impress his mates. Bloody fool.

Andy watched for a moment, judged that he wouldn't make it across the road in time and so stood back slightly from the kerb, waiting for the car to speed past. Then, he shifted his gaze slightly and saw the two boys. Both were stood just back from the road and both were looking right at him with a curious, faint, disturbing smile whispering across their lips. As he watched, they both took two short paces forward and, without ever taking their eyes from his, they calmly stepped out in front of the car.

In truth it was immaterial how fast the car was going. When the two boys suddenly appeared a few feet from the front bumper, there was no way the driver – who was, as Andy had guessed, a youth barely rid of his L plates – could ever have avoided a collision. Nevertheless, instinct took over when the brain had already accepted the inevitability of events. His arms jerked of his own volition and slewed the car around, not sufficiently to avoid the children, but more than enough to send it spinning across the road straight into Andy as he stood, transfixed, at the edge of the pavement.

The last thing he saw before the car ploughed into him was the two boys, stood calmly in the middle of the road beyond the careering car that should surely have ended their lives. Looking straight at him. And smiling.

In the control centre, Don had received the phone call from his nephew with less enthusiasm than he would once have expected. Like Andy, over the last few weeks, he had become disenchanted with the prospects of ever finding a solution to the problem. Unlike Andy, he was also not overly excited about actually achieving their goal. There remained a nagging doubt about the nature of the manifestations they were seeking to reveal. To a large extent this was borne out of the fact that he knew so very little about them beyond the mere fact of their existence. Whilst he continued to find comfort in the reasoning that they had clearly been a part of the history of the town for a considerable period of time with no apparent adverse effects, there remained that dark kernel of fear in the deepest recesses of his mind that saw the solution to this riddle as not a triumph but a disaster. Why, he could not honestly say. But the feeling remained and, just like these ghostly figures, it haunted him.

It took several minutes to get the system back on line and the pictures from the cameras back onto the monitors. He had added extra monitors over the last few weeks so that he could watch more of the streets without having to switch between cameras on the same screen. This improvement had been something he had been suggesting for years now and so when he started to make the additions no one else really thought it odd. They just assumed that he had finally been given permission and, more importantly, the budget. In fact, the extra monitors were screens that Don and Andy had put together, after raiding the council's collection of redundant and scrap electronics waiting in some storeroom to be disposed of, under some newfangled Brussels recycling regulation. Since they had already been stacked there for more than a year, it was long past the point where anyone would notice if anything went missing.

So, as he now took his place in his seat with his back to the door, Don was faced with a bank of no less than nine monitors, all oriented so that the slightest shift of the head or glance could bring the screen into focus. His colleague on shift with him that evening had disappeared some twenty minutes before, mumbling about going to get a sandwich from the garage on North Street. Don knew that he would be tucked away in a nest somewhere in the basement of the building, catching an hour's sleep whilst the building was otherwise empty. It was not something you would ever catch Don doing, nor something he approved of, but on this occasion it did at least give him the opportunity to review the operation of the enhanced cameras without the constant barrage of useless enquiries and inane comments.

As he brought each monitor on line he felt a slight frisson of excitement, which turned rapidly to wonder and tremulous delight. In spite of the late hour, on each and every camera there was at least one figure, strolling across the town square, chatting outside the bank, gazing into shop windows or sitting on the park benches. It was not the mere presence of these figures which gave him such a deep rumbling, churning thrill. It was the fact that, on the last two monitors, both of which were linked to normal, unmodified cameras showing scenes across the park and the market place, there was not a single person to be seen.

Instinctively under his breath he whispered his mantra.

"I can see you. I can see you all."

They had done it. He had done it. The camera filters had worked and, for the first time he was able to see and, more importantly, record the existence of these phantom figures who had, for so long, defied normal electronic observation.

Hardly daring to take his eyes from the monitors for fear that when he looked back the figures would have disappeared, he reached out and felt about for his mobile phone which he knew was sat on the desk to his right. He must tell Andy. He must show him what the cameras had revealed.

Then, as his hand closed around the phone, he hesitated and held his breath. Something stirred in the shadows on every camera. As he watched in growing horror, more and more of the previously invisible figures were appearing on the monitors. Some were walking out of locked doorways, some were coming into view round corners, some were simply materialising out of empty night air in the middle of the street or evolving out of the shadows, seeming to grow into human form from the darkness itself. Dozens of people, hundreds of people, thousands of people. They filled every street, every pathway. On every camera, tens of thousands of them. All standing, silent, waiting.

He said it again, but this time with far less conviction, his breath sucking in and out of his lungs with a sharp rattle like shingle on the beach as fear overcame him...

"I can see you... I can..."

It was then that Don realised he was not alone. There was someone beside him, just behind his right shoulder. Someone, or something.

In that same instant he also knew that no one could possibly have entered the room. The door had remained silent. It had not squeaked. It had made not a single sound. And yet, there was someone leaning over right by his shoulder and whispering poisonously in his ear. A sibilant hiss; ancient, corrupt and utterly inhuman.

And as it spoke, every face on every screen turned to look directly at him, looking right through the cameras into the office where he sat. Staring and faintly, maliciously, smiling. Echoing the whisper that formed the last words he would ever hear. The whisper that slipped into his mind and brought with it the everlasting darkness.

"And we can see you".

A Change for The Better

Whilst I have used many people I know as the basis for characters in my tales, A Change For The Better was the first story that was directly inspired by two of my friends. There is something of a competition now amongst friends and colleagues, to be killed off in the most novel fashion in one of these stories and the waiting list of people wanting to suffer a literary fate worse than death seems to grow daily. Which just goes to show that whatever weirdness writers can dream up for their stories, real life will always be there waiting to go one better.

As if to prove that point, just a few months after I finished this tale, we moved into a Georgian house with a skylight which bore an uncanny similarity to the one described in the story. On cold, clear winter's nights, when the moonlight shines straight down through the skylight into the deserted hallway and every shadow seems laden with menace, I reveal the true colour of the blood that beats through the veins of every writer of supernatural fiction.

I stay in bed, hide under the covers and try not to wake the kids with my whimpers.

A Change for the Better

By the time she reached her fortieth birthday, Mrs Diana Appleby was finally free of all the distractions that career or motherhood might bring into an otherwise restful life. Her twin daughters had each found young, eligible suitors and had flown the nest as soon as socially acceptable. Her son was away at university and was not expected to return until he ran out of money. And her husband provided an income which ensured there was no need for the mistress of the house to think about taking on even the slightest of part time employment. She was, in short, a lady of leisure.

And she loathed it.

Whilst she harboured no illusions about her station in life she was, nevertheless, well-educated and of above average intelligence, and the prospect of spending the next forty years or so as, what her mother jokingly referred to as, 'a lady wot lunches', filled her with the most absolute dread. For months she cast around for some project that would satisfy her – something that would do more than just pass the time, something that would provide a real challenge and allow her to stretch her abilities and prove that she was more than just a dumb blonde, incapable of even the simplest of tasks.

Diana had tried all the typical pastimes that were associated with her social position. She had joined the Women's Institute, had shown her vegetables, her flowers and her outlandish arrangements that looked like they had been treated with arsenic before going on display. She had travelled up to London for courses on interior design and into Aldwark for evening classes on Local History, Literary Appreciation and Watercolour Painting. It is a credit to her abilities that, flower arranging accepted, she had been more than capable in all these pastimes. But therein lay the problem. None of these recreations really challenged her abilities nor stimulated her interest for more than a week or two. What she needed was a project. Some grand scheme that would challenge her sufficiently to maintain her long-term interest and which, just as importantly, she considered to be of some practical value.

And so, after long deliberation and some judicious consultation with friends and family, she decided to build a house.

To anyone who didn't know Diana Appleby, this might have seemed an extraordinary proposition. To be sure, she certainly did not intend to build the thing with her own fair hands. Rather, it was her intention – with the rather expensive help of a top London architect – to design a house of which she would then supervise the construction, using only the finest craftsmen brought in from across the shire. The house would be a shining example of what could be achieved by an educated and emancipated modern lady.

Of course, first she needed to find a suitable plot of land. Setting is everything when building a dream home. No matter how fine the architecture, the most potentially sublime of houses is little more than a pile of carefully arranged bricks if the lands within which it sits are not equally delightful. Unfortunately this first obstacle proved considerably more difficult to overcome than Diana would have anticipated. A desire to build close to or within her own village of Long Benton was driven by the need for her to be on site each and every day in a supervisory capacity. She had no faith that even the finest of builders and craftsmen would not look for ways to save money and so improve their profits by cutting corners, and she was determined that this would not be allowed to occur on her project. In addition, the design of the building was anything but straightforward and she anticipated many discussions and disagreements as to the best way to bring her ideas to fruition. For these and other, more prosaic, reasons she was insistent that her new house should be built within easy walking distance of her current home.

Unfortunately, Long Benton was bounded to the east and south by the slow curve of the River Withy, whilst to the west the extensive, manicured lands of Shorlton Hall prevented any development on that side of the village. To the north, the vistas were most unappealing and the low lying marshy ground generated humours which were known to be inconducive to genteel health. This left very little land suitable for the large-scale project that Diana had in mind and, after much deliberation, she realised that it would be necessary to first remove some existing properties before being able to go forward with her grand designs.

The site Mrs Appleby eventually chose for her new venture was at the southern end of the village on the banks of the River Withy. Where the river turned north in a long lazy bend there was a large plot of some three acres which, when first she decided to acquire it, was occupied by an old, crumbling, Georgian style property; long abandoned and surely destined to end its days as a derelict, ivy festooned death trap which would lure unwary children to their doom in its half-collapsed stairwells and dark dismal cellars. It was a property encompassing, as the estate agent so elegantly phrased it, the most unusual and distinctive features.

Given the central role it will play in our story, it is perhaps necessary to digress for a few moments to describe more fully the stately pile that Diana Appleby was so intent on demolishing.

A large and admittedly beautifully proportioned three storey edifice, superficially built on a classical symmetrical floor plan, its tall sash windows, doors and ornate entablature were all immediately recognisable as Georgian in style. From the outside it was clear that in its day it must have been a most handsome building but years of neglect and decay and brought it low and the ivy which now covered the greater portion of its facade served much as a veil to hide its embarrassment from the rest of the world.

From the front there was little that was obviously unusual about the property or its setting. But that all changed as soon as one passed, very carefully and not without a little trepidation, through the front door. Within, all semblance of Georgian style and reserve was abandoned. It was as if the original architect was paying only lip service to the conventions of the day, constructing a conventional shell within which he could allow his own crazed ideas to take shape hidden from public view.

The rooms of the ground floor all had a vaguely functional feel to them most unlike anything that would be found in a family home. There was little sense of comfort; corridors were narrow, winding and ill lit;

rooms large, stone flagged or tiled and showing no sign of ever having been decorated, with bare, unplastered stone walls throughout.

The dining room and kitchen both had the air of a refectory and other reception rooms were notable by their absence. The whole place was quite extraordinarily dark, dank and cold and there was little to indicate it had ever been otherwise even when occupied. The high ceilings, ill lit and festooned in cobwebs, did nothing to alleviate this impression.

On the eastern side of the house was a room which received no natural daylight. From the outside there appeared to be windows but a cursory inspection revealed these to be false, presumably the result of an attempt to avoid the window taxes which had been prevalent when the building was originally constructed. Whatever the reason, the effect clearly suited the architect who had designed this dark, secretive chamber as a chapel. That, at least, appeared to have been its intended function. At the north end was a raised stone platform upon which an altar had presumably once stood, whilst traces of pews, long since removed and presumably burnt, still scarred the flagged floor.

The rear half of the house was occupied by a large, panelled library, filled with heavy wooden shelves now long bereft of books. But even without its vital contents the function of the room could never have been in doubt. High windows covered in thick, almost opaque, glass cast weak, filtered natural light upon the wooden stacks, catching every mote of dust that floated through the room, disturbed from its resting place by the heavy footfalls and clumsy fumblings of the unwelcome visitors.

And that was the overriding feeling that one got from the house in general and this large, desolate room in particular. Visitors – intruders – were most definitely not welcome. It was, of course, nothing obvious. There were no overt signs, no mysterious noises nor even an impression of general malignancy. Instead the overwhelming feeling about the place was one of righteous indignation much as one would receive having wandered into someone's back garden on a Sunday as they sat at afternoon tea. The house did not feel threatening, just peeved.

Nor, in spite of the surprise that awaited above, did this impression diminish as one carefully climbed the large central staircase that rose from the entrance hall to the first floor. If the ground floor was a dark, dank place of labyrinthine corridors and shadowed rooms then, in contrast, the first floor was nothing short of a revelation. Consisting of a single vast room, it was a place of dancing sunlight filtered through the dust of many decades of neglect. An echoing void which induced a momentary feeling of agoraphobia after the constraining darkness of the rooms below, the space was broken only by ornately decorated stone columns which emerged – one might almost say grew – from deep within the oak floor to support the high, arched ceiling. Whilst there were no partitions to break up the space, the arrangement of these columns, running parallel to the walls, served to produce an effect similar to that of a cloister with covered passageways surrounding a larger open area – almost a courtyard – in the centre of the room.

As with the rest of the house, time had left its corrosive mark upon the room with rotting timbers, crumbling plaster and broken windows. The centre of the floor above had partially collapsed in a mouldering heap of plaster and lathe, and pigeons had coated every surface in a thick white layer of feathers and guano.

Whilst again there was no feeling of malice, the whole room had an unwelcoming air. It was almost as if, like an aged lady caught out by an unexpected visitor, the house was embarrassed to be seen in such a state of disrepair.

On the uppermost storey, reached via a small staircase in the corner of the large pillared room, things were little better than they had been on the ground floor. After the open space of the floor below, there was a return to an arrangement which, once again, served only to confuse and disorient. Dark narrow corridors connected oddly shaped, wood panelled rooms whose original function could only be guessed at. Most were too small to have served as bedrooms and appeared more like cells, with room perhaps for a narrow bed and little else. Ceilings were low and windows, where present, small and incapable of casting much more than a thin token shaft of pale light upon the interior. As with the rest of the house there was little or no sign of decoration or comfort and not one single piece of furniture or fitting, personal artefact or forgotten scrap that would confirm that anyone had ever lived in these depressing, forgotten chambers. There was an air of damp and desolation about the whole place and no one who ventured onto the upper floor doubted for a moment that the best thing to be done was to tear it all down and start again.

Returning, oh so very carefully, to the ground floor and proceeding via a small door set low into the wall to the rear of the kitchens, one found oneself descending a set of steep, narrow and decidedly precipitous rough brick-built stairs into the depths below the house. Here the stone flagged cellar rooms were large, high ceilinged and well ventilated, yet oppressive. Surprisingly, given the proximity to the river and the decrepit state of the rest of the property, the cellars were dry and showed little sign of decay beyond the smell of musty dampness so often associated with subterranean constructions.

The extent of the cellars was difficult to ascertain but it was obvious that they were at least as large as the overlying house and it appeared that they followed the floorplan of a much earlier and more sprawling building, since at times they extended far beyond the bounds of the Georgian pile above. No one could be found from amongst the surveyors who was willing to map the limits of the subterranean rooms and passages and it was a matter of only a few minutes consideration for Mrs Appleby and her architect to decide that the best course of action was to pump the whole lot full of concrete.

After such a long period of abandonment there was little sign of even the most basic of decoration in the house, but the whole place gave the impression of having been a stark and foreboding habitation even when it was new.

Throughout the whole shadowed edifice there was no sign of either gas lighting nor the electricity which had been installed in most of the properties and certainly in all of the larger, wealthier houses in the village by the end of the first decade of the new century. Indeed, it appeared that the only source of light that had ever been used were candles and rush torches, whose brackets still adorned walls on the ground and first floors. In spite of its outward Georgian facade, the house had a positively medieval air about it.

Perhaps the most unusual feature was on the roof. Unlike all the other houses in the village this was flat, solidly built and surrounded by a low balcony so that one could reasonably walk in safety upon it. At least, one would have been able to when they house was inhabited. As is so often the way with such things, it had suffered terribly down through the decades that the building had been left abandoned. In two places, undermined by woodworm and rot from beneath and weighed down by standing water from above, the roof had given way completely and collapsed into the maze of tiny rooms and corridors on the floor below. In others it was buckled and warped as if the whole building had been twisted and bent by some malevolent and unnatural force. Its high points overgrown with moss and grasses whilst its troughs held pools of stagnant brown water, it provided little shelter for the rooms below and was a death trap for anyone now foolish enough to venture out onto its wide exposed surface.

Only one section of the roof still maintained any semblance of integrity. In the south-eastern corner, towards the rear of the building, there stood out from the roof a large, quite extraordinary domed room which gave bore a strong resemblance to an astronomical observatory. Constructed of an ornate, wrought iron skeleton infilled with glass – some plain, some stained – its weight was such that it had apparently been necessary to reinforce walls and beams of the rooms below and this, combined with the protection from the elements provided by the structure itself, had prevented the deterioration of the roof to the same degree as had been inflicted on the rest of the building.

As to the age and purpose of this remarkable room, there was no clue in either its construction nor those few fittings which remained within. Largely bare, the interior wall of the structure was adorned with many iron clips, hooks and clamps but of what these had once held there was no remnant or sign. Otherwise the strange glasshouse contained only one notable feature. Standing in the very centre of the single domed room was a large, undecorated, cup shaped frame constructed, like its surroundings, of blackened wrought iron which supported and contained a lens of the darkest, smoke hued glass. When first seen from the gap which had once contained the door to the room, it resembled nothing so much an enormous free-standing shaving mirror. The lens was able to rotate freely in all directions within the frame although the cursory examination made during the initial survey of the house failed to reveal any detail of the mechanism by which this was achieved. Nor did it shed any light on the purpose to which this lens might have been devoted.

Mrs Appleby made only one visit to the roof of the house prior to its demolition and this in direct response to the news afforded to her by the surveyors concerning this strange room and its singular contents. So taken was she by what she assumed was an art nouveau structure, that she gave orders for it to be carefully dismantled and brought down from its lofty position so that it could be reconstructed in the garden of her future home as a folly cum summer house.

There was one other feature of note which left visitors to the house both slightly awed and more than a little disturbed, though the reason for the latter feeling was never something anyone could clearly articulate. Although, as previously noted, the house was generally bereft of decoration there was one notable exception to be found, perhaps appropriately as it would turn out, in the dining room.

Having made the briefest of mentions of this feature we shall now leave it with the promise to return later in the company of an addition to the cast of our story, a certain Mr Christopher Smithers, who now strides onto centre stage for the first time.

From very early on in the project, Mrs Appleby's husband Paul had been concerned by his wife's plans. Whilst he would never have considered anything as radical as preventing Diana from pursuing her ambitions, knowing the manner in which she tended to throw herself body and soul into her schemes, he was nevertheless concerned that she might overstretch herself either physically, emotionally or, perhaps most worryingly, financially. As the weeks passed and he became more and more disturbed by the intensity with which his wife was committing herself to the project, he strove to find some way in which he could lighten the mood. Unable, due to the pressures of his own work, to take an active role in the venture he had finally settled upon a scheme of his own to show his support for her work. To this end he had, without his wife's knowledge, retained the services of Smithers, a local antiquarian, to produce a brief history of the site in the form of a simple bound booklet. He hoped that this little memento would help perhaps in inspiring Diana in her obvious struggle to complete the project in a fashion with which she could be content.

Expecting there to be little information to work with, the antiquarian, a rotund, balding and somewhat aging, but still energetic former verger, embarked on a programme of research in local libraries and the Shire Records

Office. And in very short order he found far more than he had anticipated.

Smithers made a point of reporting his progress to his client once a week, generally on a Thursday evening when it could be assured that Mrs Appleby would be occupied with matters related to her position as secretary of the local Women's Institute – the only distraction she had allowed herself from the building project, and that only because she had been unable to find anyway to escape her duties. From the first, the antiquarian was able to provide Mr Appleby with a steady stream of interesting minor facts and snippets of history relating to the house and its site. But he chose not to reveal too much, as it was his intention to present his work in a finished form by the close of the year. Indeed, the Thursday evening meetings served more as an opportunity for a quiet glass or two of port and an amiable discussion of matters entirely unrelated to Mrs Appleby's project. Most commonly, the evening was spent turning over the latest troublesome news from the sub-continent or the lamentable performance of the England cricket team on its latest tour to the colonies.

But all the while Smithers continued his researches and all the while his disquiet grew. As the first obscure references to the house were unearthed, the seed of a terrible idea which had long ago taken root in his mind was allowed to germinate and put forth sickly, invasive shoots. From that point forward, at every turn and with every new tiny grain of evidence he uncovered, the roots and rhizomes of this parasitic idea spread and infected every part of his thinking. As time slipped by and the seasons turned from spring to summer, the antiquarian became convinced that there was something deeply, desperately wrong with the site that his client's wife had chosen for her new home.

And while Smithers continued his research and slowly picked away at the history of the benighted plot of land, he kept a weather eye towards the site where, equally slowly, the destruction of the old building commenced.

From the start it was a task filled with frustration and setback. Anything and everything that could go wrong did. Sickness, accidents, theft, misplaced equipment and supplies. At every turn it seemed that there was an unseen force doing its utmost to prevent the destruction of the old house. Most seriously it proved impossible to fill in the cellars. However much concrete was pumped down, it simply seemed to disappear into previously unnoticed voids leaving the original chambers almost empty. After three attempts, the combined costs of which threatened to bankrupt the whole project before it had even really started, Diana and her architect were forced to admit defeat and alter the plans for the new house to take into account the continued existent of the ancient subterranean spaces.

The problems continued as the wreckers moved in and the final deconstruction of the old house commenced. At times the pace of the dismemberment was so painfully slow that it seemed it would have been quicker just to leave the place alone and let nature take its course. It was as if the house itself was resisting any and all attempts to hasten its final collapse. By the time the roof had been removed, the work foreman, Brigham, an old, gnarled trunk of a man whose skin had been weathered to the colour of saddle leather by a lifetime of exposure to the sun and wind, was reporting that fully half of his entire workforce had quit and that the rest were demanding danger money before they would even consider going back on the site. Monies paid from an ever-shrinking budget, the destruction continued at the same glacial pace. Faced with the continued failure of machines to function correctly within the bounds of the site, there was little alternative but to take down the walls of the house brick by brick. Though this did have the unexpected advantage of allowing Mrs Appleby the opportunity of having them cleaned and stacked ready for reuse in the new building – something which would save a considerable sum of money but which she had vehemently opposed when it had originally been suggested.

Nor was this the only decision made by Diana which seemed at odds with both the original plans and her long held and much discussed views on almost every aspect of the new house. It was as if the brick by brick demolition of the old property was matched by a similar demolition of all her most trenchant beliefs and ideas. By the time the site was finally cleared and prepared for the new building phase, Diana's mind resembled a similarly blank canvas, seemingly bereft of ideas and awaiting inspiration. The question that worried Smithers as he continued his lonely researches was where exactly that inspiration would originate.

And so it continued through the summer. The site was finally cleared of the last remnants of the building, of which nothing remained above ground but the neat stacks of bricks and worked stone stored beneath canvas along the river bank. And of course the strange ironwork structure that had been rescued from the roof and now sat incongruously in the middle of the neglected lawns.

Mrs Appleby had hoped that the long awaited and much delayed demolition of the Georgian house would have eased her mind, providing her with that long sought after clean slate upon which to realise her designs. But the spirit of the house had long experience of protecting itself and although its power may have been diminished by the destruction of its physical form, that did not mean that it was without subtle weapons which it could utilise to protect itself and ensure that, in the end, it would win out. So it was that, each time she surveyed the now empty site, Diana could not help but superimpose an image of the lost house upon the scene. It seemed clear that the building, or the power that had long dwelt within it, was not intent on letting go and would frustrate all her attempts to bring her own designs to fruition.

In August, construction commenced on the new house with what, in the light of the snail's pace to date, might be considered surprising alacrity. Outwardly at least, it appeared that the ghosts of the previous building had finally been exorcised, and within a few short weeks the walls were up to the second storey window level and thoughts were turning to the roof and to starting to fit out the interior. And yet at the same time it was clear that things were not as harmonious as they first appeared. Shortly before building started, Diana sacked the architect who had hitherto been her staunchest advocate and supporter in the project. The stated cause of the rift was one of money, although to her closest friends Mrs Appleby confided that she had had to let the man go as he was stifling her creativity. She claimed that his 'mundane application of outdated concepts' was preventing her from creating an architectural masterpiece. Whilst he might dispute the exact way in which she phrased it, the architect would probably have agreed that 'creative differences' lay at the heart of the dispute. Put simply, he was of the opinion that his former client was rapidly losing her mind and he had no wish to be associated with the monstrosity she was proposing to build. In light of the way in which events subsequently unfolded, it would not be an exaggeration to say that this was the best decision he would ever make. It was one that, in all likelihood, saved both his sanity and, ultimately, his life.

And so the work continued. The only person that Diana Appleby would now trust with any of her decisions was the foreman of the works, Brigham. It was he who organised and executed all the technical details of the construction and who followed his mistress's instructions to the letter. Indeed, it seemed that he was as deeply affected by the pernicious influence of the house as his employer and at times was almost able to sense her needs and instructions without a word being spoken; if, in fact, they were her instructions at all.

As for the workforce, no one now remained of the original team who had been hired to complete the demolition and rebuilding of the house. All had fallen by the wayside in one way or another, either through illness, accident, exhaustion or simply failing to turn up for work. In spite of the extra pay being promised, no one lasted more than a couple of weeks on the site. There was a constant turnover of workers, with those lucky enough to escape unharmed refusing to discuss either what they had seen or why they had chosen to leave such a lucrative job. On any normal project such a turnover of skilled men would have resulted in chaos. But of course this was no normal project, and the building programme was kept on course through the combined sheer willpower of Diana and her faithful foreman.

It was a damp, dank October afternoon and the rain spattered intermittently against the windows. Paul Appleby was reading the paper in front of the fire and considering rousing himself to some work when he heard the sharp rap of the knocker at the front door and the housekeeper's footsteps, followed by a short, muffled conversation. Deciding not to wait on Mrs Watkins' announcement, he rose and walked through into the hall to ascertain the identity of the visitor. He was somewhat surprised to see the antiquarian, Smithers, hunched up against the weather and clutching a large canvas bag, stood on the doorstep.

"I am sorry to disturb you, Mr Appleby. I was wondering if I might have a few minutes of your time to discuss the work you commissioned?"

Appleby frowned momentarily, not unkindly but as if the historian's presence had reminded him of something unpleasant. It was only a fleeting expression and it passed almost as quickly as it had appeared but Smithers, already conscious of the disturbing nature of the news he would reveal, noticed it nonetheless.

"Of course, Mr Smithers, do come in."

The short, round visitor edged his way past the housekeeper and followed his host, not into the sitting room from where Mr Appleby had appeared and where they had conducted their previous business, but through into the dining room whose large bow windows would usually, on better days than this, present fine views of the garden and the fields beyond.

"Let me get some tea rustled up and we can have a look at what you have to show me."

Appleby pulled a cord by the door and a bell could be heard ringing somewhere in the back of the house. Almost immediately footsteps again echoed in the hallway and the housekeeper appeared to receive instructions. Once he had ordered up tea, the younger man unceremoniously dragged out a chair at the head of the table and sank into it with a sigh as if at the end of a long day's exertion.

"I think this would be the best place to talk. The table is large enough for your portfolio and the light is the best to be had in the house though," he glanced out of the window, "today that is perhaps not saying much. I had a fire laid in here before lunch as I intended spending the afternoon doing some accounts, so we should be quite warmed against the rather dismal day."

Smithers took his place facing the large windows and began to unpack his documents.

"Of course, of course. Again, apologies for the early hour. I would, by choice, have come to present my news this evening but I know you would rather your wife was not aware of your gift until the appropriate moment. Since I noticed she was down at the new house when I passed there this afternoon, I thought it the ideal time to update you on progress and discuss a few matters which are causing me a little... well, a little concern shall we say."

Appleby sighed and stroked his brow. Seemingly ignoring his guest, he turned in his chair to look through the rain spattered window and muttered almost as if to himself.

"Why am I not surprised? Everything about that accursed house seems to give cause for more than just a little concern."

He turned back towards the older man and continued.

"So tell me, Mr Smithers. What horrors have you found out about the benighted place? How much am I going to regret ever having agreed to this crazed plan of my wife's?"

Smithers smiled wanly, his forced light-heartedness revealing rather more about his unease than he had intended. "Well I think that perhaps 'horrors' is too strong a word..." he hesitated as Appleby snorted, "...but it certainly has a colourful history and there are some, well, some unusual matters which I thought should be brought to your attention. If you have the time I would like to briefly run over what I have uncovered about the property. It does have a long and quite remarkable history."

"Yes, yes, do go ahead."

Appleby was displaying an unusual irritability, out of character for a man widely admired for his tolerance and patience. Smithers guessed that his wife's much discussed obsession with the seemingly unending project had become something of a point of tension between the otherwise well-disposed couple.

A fastidious man, well suited to research, Smithers had carefully laid out all the papers, plans and maps upon the polished oak table and, drawing out a large notebook, secured with blue ribbon and looking very much like an accountant's leather-bound ledger, he began to explain his findings.

"The first reference I have found to the house – well actually to the land itself – comes in a grant from the King... that would be William Rufus, the Conqueror's son, to Herbert de Benton in 1094. It was he, de Benton I mean, not the King of course, who gave his name to the village. Obviously there had been something here before, in Saxon times, but we seem to have lost trace of what it was called. Anyway, we know that de Benton owned the land down by the river, as it is described in some detail in the document which concerns permission to build a castle – one of those Motte and Bailey jobbies – for the purpose of controlling some rather rebellious locals who had apparently been causing a bit of grief for de Benton."

Appleby, in spite of his preoccupations, was doing his best to show interest in the historian's narrative and was genuinely surprised to hear that his wife was building her new house on the site of an ancient fortification.

"So you are telling me that there were the remains of a whole castle somewhere under that Georgian ruin?"

"Well, it wouldn't have been a very big castle, even had it been finished, just a large mound with a palisade on top I expect. But in any event, it was never completed. Apparently there was some sort of religious establishment – I presume a church or perhaps a monastery – on the site and de Benton was foolish enough to knock it down and try and stick his keep on top of it. It was quite common back then. In some cases, whole quarters of towns were knocked down to accommodate the new castle. I think there was something of a point being made if you see what I mean."

"Anyway, it seems that the locals took great exception to having their church or monastery built over and there was something of an uprising. There are not that many details, but it appears that de Benton's response was rather extreme, and all trace of the village disappears for almost two hundred years. Strangely though, de Benton never did finish the castle he had started and concentrated on his manor instead – what later became Shorlton Hall."

Smithers was picking over the documents, pamphlets and plans as he spoke, illustrating each statement by distractedly waving the relevant piece of paper briefly at his host before returning it to the table and glancing back at his notebook for inspiration as he continued his narrative. In spite of his previous sour mood, Appleby found the man's enthusiasm most endearing and was himself warming to the subject.

"There are a few references throughout the thirteenth and early fourteenth centuries, mostly tithes and tax documents. Thanks heavens for the greed of the church and the king eh," the historian laughed quietly at his own little joke, "and it seems that your site had once again returned to the service of the Lord – the heavenly one I mean rather than the temporal – since there was by now a well-established Abbey on the site. Not very rich nor popular with the pilgrims, by all accounts, but getting by all the same. There might have been some Templar connection, but the evidence is slight and, to be honest, round here almost every church barn is claimed to have been used by the Templars so I don't set much stead by that."

"But it does seem that the Abbey and the village were continuing to suffer some rather bad luck. All the records I could find make continual reference to applications for a waiver of tithes and taxes due to various mishaps, bad harvests, fires, plagues, robberies or floods. Come the Black Death in 1349 and the whole place almost ceased to exist again."

"There is nothing at all recorded about the village for the next couple of hundred years. Well almost nothing anyway. Hardly surprising given that so many places just vanished forever after the great plague. Nobody left to work the fields, nobody left to buy the crops even if they could produce it. A third of the population dead, thousands of settlements just vanished, nothing more than a few ditches and banks left in the landscape. Very sad. Very sad indeed."

Smithers hesitated in his story, lost momentarily in thought as he absent-mindedly removed his spectacles, took out a handkerchief and cleaned the lenses before carefully replacing them on the bridge of his nose and proceeding once again.

"That might have happened to Long Benton as well, except of course... well, except it didn't, did it. As we know."

The strange little man chuckled somewhat self-consciously to himself before continuing with his history lesson.
"We have only one oblique reference to Long Benton in the whole of the fifteenth century and that took me an age and a whole bucket full of luck to find. I was searching through all the deeds and land registries, the charters and legal rulings and getting absolutely nowhere. Days I spent at the archives, trying to find any trace that would give a clue as to the fate of the village

those two hundred or so years from the middle of the fourteenth century up to the arrival of Good King Harry. Not a sausage. I was convinced that the whole place had been abandoned after the plague. And then. Aha!!"

The rotund fellow became disturbingly animated all of a sudden and started rustling through his papers.

"Where is it, where…is… it…ah yes, here, here it is."

He was brandishing a piece of parchment tied round with black ribbon.

"Spence at the archives let me borrow it so you could see for yourself what is written. This is where things start to get… interesting."

Appleby raised one eyebrow ironically.

"Really? I was wondering when that would happen."

Smithers appeared not to have heard the slight rebuke and continued unabashed.

"Yes, yes. Now where are we. Are yes. Here you see."

He carefully unrolled the parchment to reveal a plain, undecorated, slightly browned sheet covered in fine script. Appleby rose from his chair to stand by the antiquarian but this did little to improve his ability to decipher the tiny writing.

"Now then, this is an act of attainder you see. You know what that is? No? right, well, when someone commits a serious crime against the king, rebellion, treason or suchlike, then when he is brought to justice, or even if he is already dead, he can have all his lands and goods seized by the crown. This is called attainder and this," he indicated to the parchment before them, "this is the act of attainder against a certain John de la Benton, a minor Yorkist earl who took part in a rebellion against Henry Tudor in the late fifteenth century. 1487 if I remember rightly. Lost, of course. The last battle was fought not far from here, just outside Aldwark on the Old Straight Road. Quite a messy affair by all accounts."

"Anyway, this act of attainder is the list of lands, goods and titles seized from Benton after the battle. Or rather from his family. He was already presumed dead. Never found his body, but it was probably swept up into a mass grave along with all the other poor souls who died that day."

Appleby watched as Smithers carefully traced the act, searching for the relevant text to present to his host, all the time maintaining his commentary on what he was seeking.

"Now, the thing is that most of these acts follow the same basic formula. 'Whereas Sir So And So has been found guilty of the crime of high treason against his majesty our sovereign liege etc etc.' They then proceed to outline the crimes of the poor feller who is being punished and follow that up by stating that all his worldly goods and titles are seized by the crown to be redistributed as the King sees fit. Sometimes they will list specific lands and titles but usually it is just taken as read that everything the traitor had now becomes the property of the King. Quite straight forward really. A good way for the King to get his hands on that half of Buckinghamshire he was keen on."

He laughed half-heartedly at his own joke.

"Except," he was scanning rapidly down the page, following each line with a fingertip that hovered just above the surface, "this one is different. Ah yes, here we are."

The small man moved back to allow his host sight of the ancient document, keeping his finger on a point towards the bottom of the page.

"See there. Now what do you make of that?"

Appleby leant forward to peer at the parchment. In truth, the combination of the poor light and his less than perfect eyesight meant he could read little of what was written there and understood even less. But he did not want to disappoint the little historian and so made suitably impressed noises.

"Oh yes, very interesting, very good. Well done."

He straightened from the table and looked expectantly at his guest who appeared somewhat nonplussed at this response.

"You see, don't you?" Smithers persisted.

"Er, not exactly, no. What exactly is it you are showing me."

The antiquarian jabbed his finger down on the parchment again.

"There, that last clause. Did you read what it says?"

Appleby thought he was going to have to confess his ignorance but as he leant forward once again to examine the indicated passage he was saved by Smithers' impatience. The older man plucked the paper from under his nose and recited it to the room.

"In so far as we have received representations from our bishops and other notable gentlemen of good standing, we hereby order that the lands and holdings in the parish of Benton be scourged of all souls residing therein and be delivered into the safekeeping of the Abbot of Newhouse in the hope that he may cleanse the land of the evil that has befallen it. To this end he shall be allowed any manner of authority as may be deemed necessary to expunge the malevolent power that currently resides therein."

Carefully rolling the parchment and retying the black ribbon, he placed the document back on the table and turned to Appleby.

"So what," he asked, "do you make of that?"

Appleby was silent for a moment as he digested the words of the declaration. That short paragraph, with its intimation of some malevolent evil had changed the whole tone of the meeting, and he suddenly felt quite chilled in spite of the fire that continued to crackle in the grate. He moved back round the table and carefully sat back into his chair before answering.

"It sounds... worrying. Suddenly I start to realise there might be some basis to these unexplained concerns I have had about this whole project. I think I need to know more. Tell me, tell me it all. Start with the people mentioned there. Most of those names I didn't recognise. Who was the Abbot of Newhouse and why did the King give this village to him. Have you been able to ascertain that from your studies?"

Smithers sat down in one of the high-backed chairs opposite his host on the other side of the fireplace. He leant forward slightly with his elbows resting on the arms of the chair and regarded Appleby over the top of his spectacles.

"Newhouse was an Abbey founded in these parts by the Norbertines, or to give them their proper title, the Premonstratentians. They were a monastic order who came to England in the twelfth century, 1143 to be precise, and Newhouse was their first and most important abbey."

"So they were monks then." Appleby interjected.

"Not exactly, no. The White Friars were rather different to the other monastic orders of the time. They didn't stay in their monasteries but went out amongst the flock to provide pastoral care in the parishes. As such they were somewhat - now how shall I describe it - somewhat more worldly in their affairs and their knowledge than the other orders."

"Sorry," Appleby interrupted again, "White Friars?"
"Oh yes, that is how they were known on account of their white habits."

The younger man was impressed. "You certainly seem to have done your research well, Mr Smithers."

Smithers smiled. "Oh this is not research, at least not anything you have been paying me for. One of my main areas of interest, the one that drew me into the antiquarian studies all those years ago, was ecclesiastical history. It is something of a passion for me. That is why I am so disturbed by this unexpected turn of events." The smile faded from his lips as he finished speaking.

"Anyway, the White Friars were, it seems, tasked with removing some great evil from this little village of ours. I have spent many hours these last few weeks in the library at Southwold Minster trying to hunt down any record of the nature of this evil, but I am afraid I have found almost nothing."

Appleby looked confused. "Southwold? Why there? I thought you said these White Friars were from Newhouse?"

Now that he was apparently approaching the dénouement of his story, Smithers looked slightly annoyed at this diverting interruption.

"Oh they were, just as I said. But of course, Henry Tudor's son, good King Harry, went and dissolved the monasteries in the late fifteen thirties and all the records that weren't destroyed were collected by his chancellor, Thomas Cromwell, who deposited them in a secret library at one of the few religious centres in these shires to escape the worst excesses of the reformation...?"
"...Southwold Minster!" Appleby smiled, pleased at finally making the link.

"Exactly," declared the antiquarian. "The library is said to contain many documents too important to destroy but containing information too dangerous to be allowed to become common knowledge. Its very existence was only a whispered rumour until about sixty years ago. Even today, whilst it is no longer actively hidden from view, very few people outside of a circle of ecclesiastical scholars know about it. And given the nature of the secrets protected by those walls it is perhaps best it remains that way."

Appleby sat upright. "You have my word, Mr Smithers, I shall breathe not a word of this to anyone."

He reached over for his tea, which sat on the small table at his side, but noticed the cup was half empty and what fluid remained had cooled so much as to be unpalatable. He thought for a moment and then made a decision.

"I say old chap. It's after four. Shall we have a snifter to help us along? I get the feeling I am going to need a stiff drink, the way this conversation is going."

"Oh, um, yes, er. Don't mind if I do. A whisky please if you have one. Just a small one. I need to keep my head about me at the moment."

Once the drinks were produced, Appleby resumed his seat before the fire and pressed home with the question that had hung on his lips for the last few minutes.

"So what was the nature of this horror then? What was it that had got these Norbertines so frightened? Did you find the answer at Southwold?"

Smithers gave an apologetic grimace which betrayed his failure.

"Unfortunately, either the records were destroyed at the time of the dissolution or they have been subsequently hidden away in a manner more thorough than I am able to overcome. I suspect the latter, since many other records from Newhouse, including those relating to almost every other piece of land in their possession, are still available for study. It is only those related to Long Benton which are missing."

Appleby looked thoroughly dejected. "So that's it then. A dead end."

"Well, not quite. You see, whilst all the documents from Newhouse had disappeared, the Southwold Library did yield up one more scrap of evidence which might help us understand something of the nature of the menace afflicting Long Benton and most particularly that piece of land that Mrs Appleby has rather rashly chosen for her new home."

If Appleby noticed or was in any way bothered by this implied criticism of his wife he gave no sign. Indeed, he had long since come to a similar conclusion regarding his wife's unhealthy obsession with her latest project.

"Go on then man. What do you have?"

The Antiquarian looked slightly embarrassed as he returned to the large oak table.
"Well then, this is where it starts to get really strange and where you might consider that I have rather lost my marbles."

He pulled out a large sheet of paper onto which was traced, in great detail, a map.

"This is the earliest map I have which shows the place. It dates to the early sixteenth century when Henry Tudor – the one who had the White Friars cleanse the village of its evil – was apparently giving serious consideration to the idea of giving Long Benton the status of a town and founding some sort of school or college here. I assume this was because the Norbertines had completed their task and the place was now ripe for reoccupation. Nothing ever came of it in the end. Maybe because the King died only a year or so later. But there were documents drawn up in preparation for granting a royal charter and one of these included a map of the Long Benton and its environs – this map to be precise."

He had taken a large magnifying glass from his jacket pocket and bent over the table looking for something on the plan.

"Now where are you...? Ah yes, there we go."

Smithers straightened up and gestured to his host. "Come, come, take a look at this."

Appleby approached the table and looked down at the map. It was clearly a representation of the lands around Long Benton. There was the Great North Road running almost straight up and down the paper. To the east was the ribbon of the River Withy running almost parallel with the road and between the two was the long, drawn out village of Long Benton with the old green to the north and the church at the southernmost tip. Admittedly there were far fewer buildings shown than existed today but that was hardly surprising. If he understood Smithers correctly then this plan had been drawn up only a few short years after the whole place was supposedly emptied of its people and subjected to who knows what strange rituals by the Norbertines. On reflection he was surprised that anywhere was left standing at all.

His gaze drifted across the map, being drawn slowly south and east. Down to the southern fringes of the village, to the land between the church and the river, just where it turned sharply from the east to the north.

There. He could see it now. There it was; the plot upon which his wife was supposedly creating her architectural gem, her perfect home.

"Do you see it Appleby? Do you?" Smithers whispered urgently at his shoulder. "Here, take the magnifying glass. Look closely. Tell me what you see."

The host took the proffered glass from his visitor and leant over, close to the table. He could already see that there was a dark smudge in the centre of the plot and, as he slipped the magnifying glass over the map and brought the shadow into focus, it resolved itself into a disturbingly familiar pattern.

Smithers left the Appleby house in the same manner as he had approached it; bearing a friendly, relaxed smile and a slightly apologetic air designed to reassure his host and hide the heavy sense of foreboding that lay deep and hard in his heart. But Appleby was anything but reassured. The revelations that had been presented to him in the comforting surroundings of his own dining room had shaken him badly, leaving him feeling lost, helpless and more than a little afraid for both the physical and spiritual wellbeing of his beloved wife. Whilst he was not entirely convinced that the antiquarian had not, in his own words, 'lost his marbles', there was certain enough circumstantial evidence and coincidence to leave Appleby deeply unsettled.

Seeing how unnerved his client had become during the course of the discussion, Smithers had done his best at the end to play down the significance of the evidence he had presented and had left promising to do his utmost to find a rational and logical explanation for events, both ancient and modern. At the close of the meeting, Appleby had at least agreed to delay any drastic action until Smithers had completed the drawing together of the last few strands of evidence. Then, if there were still unresolved concerns, Appleby would take steps to ensure that his wife's involvement with the benighted plot of land came to an abrupt conclusion.

Still, Appleby would have been even more concerned if he had seen the look of fear and sadness which fixed itself upon Smithers' visage as he wound his way home through the gathering dusk, past the site where Mrs Appleby and her builders were in the process of packing away their tools at the close of another day. If he had known the true nature and extent of the terror that held Smithers in its inexorable grip, then he would have rushed from the house that very moment and dragged Diana from the house, never to return. But some secrets are kept too well hidden and never destined to be revealed, even in death.

Though the quickest route home followed the footpath that crossed the entrance to the building site, Smithers made a point of crossing the road well in advance of that particular gate and passed by on the other side, keeping as much distance between himself and the accursed land as he possibly could. It had been the same his whole life. As a teenager he had regularly taken long circuitous routes along the main street, far away from the most direct homeward course, simply to avoid passing by that particular property. In his twenties he had convinced himself that such fears, however well founded, were ridiculous; the stuff of childhood fancy. As a result he had routinely, and against all his better judgement, forced himself to take the more direct route home along Church Lane, right past the dark, empty house. Even so he had never, in all the long years since, built up the courage to use the footpath closest to the house and had always passed by at a quick trot, or on occasion when the nights were dark and the moon shrouded by thick cloud, at full pelt as fast as his legs could carry him. He didn't pretend to understand the nature of the evil that infected that particular plot of land but he had good reason to know that it existed. He was convinced that the house, the very ground it stood upon, was cursed and his recent research had proved that this impression was far more than just a hangover from childhood nightmares.

Now, as he scurried past in the misty evening twilight, desperately trying to keep his eyes averted from the dark yawning entrance and the shadowed house beyond, he felt once again the overwhelming urge to stop and raise his gaze, to look once and for all upon the source of a lifetime of nightmares. His step faltered, slowed, halted. He stood on the edge of the pavement directly opposite the gate, his eyes cast down to the ground, waiting… building his courage… and failing. He couldn't do it. His nerve shattered and he almost fell away from the kerb, scuttling off, defeated, into the gathering night and the promise of the comforting, warm safety of his own home.

Smithers heard nothing from the Applebys for the next few days. The weather turned foul with an autumn storm whipping rain, hail and even a touch of sleet across the land. Branches were torn from trees and tiles swept from rooftops. Daylight was little more than a brief few hours of grey squalling gloom connecting long, raging nights when the thick clouds hid even the meagre pale light of the waning moon.

The antiquarian had hoped for further visits to Southwold or to the archives at Aldwark but in the end decided against venturing out and chose instead to stoke up the fire and remain at his desk, working once again through the various maps, books and documents that he had accrued during the researches of the last few months. His hope was that, in the rereading, he would be able to reappraise his conclusions, settle upon a less disturbing interpretation of the curious history of the site. Anything that would ease the nagging terrors that haunted his sweat soaked dreams and chased him from his bed into the half-light of morning with his heart hammering, fit to burst from his chest and a maniacal scream choking in his throat.

But whatever comfort he might have sought was not to be found in his papers. Whilst previously he had been able to find much of general or specific interest about the village, all the documents revealed was more and more evidence of the bloody and mysterious story of Long Benton in general and the Appleby's land in particular. It was as if, in a few days, someone had rewritten all the books which mentioned the place to portray it in the very worst light. The religious persecutions of Mary and Elizabeth, the internecine battles of the English Civil War and Jacobite plots of the early eighteenth century; all had left their crimson stain upon the village. It was the same story throughout its long and tortuous history. If there were a witch to be burnt, a highway man to be hung or a thief to be flayed for thirty miles around, you could bet that the punishment would be dispensed in

Long Benton. The place was surely accursed. It seemed it thrived on human suffering.

Finally on Saturday evening, his last hopes dashed and his nerves shredded by what he had read, Smithers picked up the phone and rang Appleby.

He had expected to hear concern in his client's voice but as Appleby began to talk there was no trace of the fear or distress that had been so apparent at the end of their last meeting.

"Evening Smithers. How are you, old chap? Keeping well? Hope you are staying out of this storm eh? Haven't seen the like of it for twenty years or more. A right hoolie and no mistake. So, what can I do for you?"

Smithers hesitated. Suddenly, in the face of such a jovial response, he was unsure of how to broach the subject of the research and his dark suspicions and fears.

"It's erm, it's about the land. About the matters we discussed on Thursday. I've, em, I've been doing some more work and I..."

"Oh that stuff." Appleby interrupted, before Smithers really had a chance to get into his stride. "Don't you worry about that old man. I went down to the house yesterday morning. Got a right bally soaking as well I can tell you. Still it was worth it. I had a chat with Diana and she put me straight on the whole thing. Showed me round the place, gave me a full tour. It's wonderful, absolutely perfect. She's done a superb job and it is better than we could ever have hoped. We are quite delighted, both of us."

Smithers listened in stunned silence.

"In fact," Appleby continued, "I'm afraid I rather let the cat out of the bag. Told her all about our little project. She was thrilled, I can tell you, and can't wait to read the book. She thinks it's a great idea."

The old antiquarian found his voice at last. "But what we spoke about? The map and the act of attainder. All the evidence. Aren't you worried about the place? I have found..."

"Ach, don't give it another thought, Smithers. You know how these things can seem when you only have a few bits and pieces to go on. You fill in the gaps with your imagination and all sorts of ghosties and ghoulies come crawling out. It's nothing, man. Just a bit of local colour that will make the book all the more exciting. Just crack on and get it all wrapped up by next Thursday evening and we can have a little celebration. What do you think?"

In truth, Smithers didn't know what to think. His mind was reeling and he desperately needed a drink. He muttered a few platitudes, confirmed that he would indeed attend, as usual, the following Thursday and dropped the receiver back into the cradle.

What had happened? How was it that in just a couple of short days Appleby could have so changed his mind over the whole affair? He said he had visited the house. That had to be it. Something had happened at the house. And not the pleasant guided tour he had claimed either. Smithers was convinced that some evil – the same evil that had for so long blighted the village – had stolen into Appleby's mind and corrupted him irrevocably, just as it had done to his wife and to so many other unfortunates before.

He poured himself a quite monstrous whisky and slumped into his chair, stretching his feet out towards the fire, momentarily losing himself in the dancing flames. When he roused himself a few minutes later, it was with a new resolve. It would be a lie to say he didn't know what to do now. He had known before he had even ended the call with Appleby that there was really only one course of action left open to him. It was something that even just a couple of days ago he would never have even contemplated but now, as his options closed down around him and he became ever more isolated, he knew that there was nothing else for it. If he wanted to find out finally, once and for all, what was happening in that house, he would have to go there.

He would, once and for all, have to overcome the gut-churning terror that welled up inside him and – he could hardly believe he was even considering this – step onto that infernal plot.

From without, Smithers had to admit that the new house was very impressive. Its style seemed to most closely resemble the Arts and Crafts school, as exemplified by the work of the celebrated architect Edwin Lutyens, whose renovations and new builds had so recently become all the rage from one end of the country to the other. This was hardly surprising given that Mrs Appleby was a devout disciple of Lutyens horticultural associate, the renowned garden designer Gertrude Jekyll. It was not, unfortunately, a style that necessarily appealed to Smithers, who found it altogether too quaint for his taste. That said, there was no denying that Mrs Appleby had overseen the creation of a very fine building and one that would surely, under any normal circumstances, become an attraction within the village. Of course, that was the problem. These were far from normal circumstances and this was far from being a normal house.

The other feature that struck Smithers, as he approached the front of the house, was the sheer size of it. From the road it had been difficult to get a clear impression of just how large the place really was but now, up close, he could see that it sprawled across an area far more extensive than the original property. In addition, and in a similar fashion to the Georgian house it had replaced, rather than just a single upper storey there were in fact two, the second being partly tucked away beneath the low-slung roof. It had taken a quite superb piece of design to manage to create this upper floor without ruining the overall proportions of the building. In spite of himself, Smithers could not help but admire the skill of both architect and builder.

The storms of the previous few days had eased to a damp, misty, chill morning which promised more rain later but which for now was at least dry enough to allow one to take a brief walk without getting soaked to the skin. Even so, being a Sunday, the site was deserted. Try as she might, even the redoubtable and often domineering Diana Appleby could not persuade the builders to give up their Sabbath in order to speed along the completion of her project. And so, much to her impatience and chagrin, for at least one day a week the house was left to its own devices.

Now why, Smithers wondered as he walked down the gravelled drive towards the front door, had he thought of it in that way? 'Left to its own devices' implied he was imbuing the house with some sort of consciousness, perhaps even some sort of intelligence. Why should he think of it in those terms? It was, after all, nothing more than an inanimate object and had no more self-awareness than the stones crunching beneath his feet. In the cold light of day, he was able to take a slightly more pragmatic view of the whole affair. He was, he concluded, letting his past experiences and his researches impart his imagination with altogether too much supposition and fanciful deduction. It was a house, built by man – or in this case woman – to her design. It had walls, a floor and a roof. It was a thing, devoid of conscious thought, malice, kindness, avarice or any other sort of human emotion.

In which case, he found himself wondering as he approached the front porch, why was he here?

With a sudden violent jerk he shook his head, as if to dislodge something that should not have been there. As he did so, his mind cleared and the fears returned. What had just happened? Had those been his thoughts? Had that misty calmness that had descended upon his mind as he approached the house been the result of his own consciousness or something else, something external, something... malignant.

The antiquarian hesitated, just a few steps short of the front entrance. Although the heavy oak door itself was fitted, it bore no lock and swung back and forth very slightly as the autumn winds whipped leaves around in a tight eddy in the open porch. It would be a matter of less than a moment for him to push open the door and step inside but, for some reason which currently escaped him, he chose instead to turn away and move towards the side of the property with the intention of completing a circuit of the exterior before venturing within.

He had never set foot upon this site before today, although he had of course passed the gated entrance - usually at something rather faster than a gentle amble - almost every day since he was a child.

Since he was a child.

There of course lay the root cause of his apprehension, his antipathy and undoubtedly his fear. As a child he had stood at the gates looking down the curved driveway towards the old house, staring at it through the trees as his two closest friends taunted him from halfway along the avenue of old, gnarled and twisted limes. He had endured their scornful laughs and resisted all their attempts to persuade him to cross that boundary and approach the sinister, tumbledown property. He had watched, unable to turn away in spite of the urge to flee, as they approached the broken down front door and were swallowed up by the dark interior. He had listened as their long screams of laughter and cries of mock horror echoed through the halls and rooms and tumbled out of the broken windows.

And finally he had caught, at the very furthest edges of his hearing, the faint, short, rattling screams of terror as the malevolent house swallowed his friends up without trace, never to be seen alive again.

It was a tragic accident of course – at least that was how it was portrayed by the authorities. When the boy's bodies were discovered a few days later, close to a drainage outflow in the nearby river, it was deduced that they had been playing a trick on their young companion but it had gone terribly wrong. Over the many years since Smithers had rationalised the traumatic events in just such a manner, accepting that any other memories or theories he might have about the deaths were the product of an overactive and scarred childhood imagination. The fear of the old house had never waned, but he had come to accept it as a part of his psyche rather than a response to anything more tangible. Until the revelations of last few months.

Cautiously moving down along the side of the house, the antiquarian stepped out onto the wide-open space between the property and the river which, once building was completed and the gardens had been replanted, would serve as the main lawn. For now it resembled nothing so much as a farmer's yard, thick with mud and pocked here and there with standing pools of rain water. The ground rose towards the river's edge where an artificial bank had been raised as flood protection. Concluding that the bank would provide a good vantage point from which to study the rear of the property, Smithers scampered quickly across the muddy ground and up onto the levee.

Turning his back on the steep drop to the water beyond, he scanned along the back of the property, looking for anything out of the ordinary, anything that might single out this particular building as being in any way unusual. At first he could see nothing. It all appeared just as it should. A little too stark and new in the landscape but the apparent reuse of old bricks and stone – he assumed from the previous house – along with the rustic design of the building, helped to tone down the newness. At first glance there was nothing at all that would so much as raise an eyebrow. At first glance.

Smithers slowly raised his eyes to the roof. Starting low over the second storey windows, the red tiled roof rose steeply and steadily towards the ridgeline. But there was something odd. The angle of the roof looked wrong – steeper than he would have expected – and it ended sooner than it should have. Put simply, the roof did not reach the centre of the house. Furthermore, there appeared to be some sort of structure, made perhaps of iron, sticking up beyond the ridgeline, though the exact nature of the feature he couldn't ascertain from where he stood.

Intrigued by what he was seeing and still keeping his eyes fixed firmly on the roof, Smithers began to slowly circle the house at a distance far enough removed to give him clear sight of the ridgeline. It was only a matter of minutes before he had returned to his original position on the bank and had, in the process, deduced that whilst the roof on all four sides rose from the walls as normal, the four sections did not, it appeared, meet in the middle. Rather, there appeared to be a rooftop courtyard in the centre of the house which contained some sort of wrought iron structure. More disturbingly, closer inspection of the walls and windows as he had circled the building had revealed many to be carefully constructed forgeries, blank brick features designed to give the appearance of being windows, but which would surely have thrown no light onto the rooms within. The aging historian's disquiet sprang forth once more. It was clear that Appleby had either been lying or delusional in his descriptions of the house. This was no home. Smithers had no clear idea what it was, but he knew that much. This was definitely no home.

Burning curiosity, verging on anger, now drove him to do something he had never thought possible. He returned to the front of the house and without a moment's further hesitation he stepped in through the door into the Stygian gloom.

Whatever concerns Smithers might have felt, as he surveyed the house from the relative safety of the garden, were transformed into outright horror as he entered the building itself. To the very last he had harboured some vague hope that he had somehow been wrong, and that the interior of the house was indeed as Appleby had described it. As he moved further in and explored the maze of dark stone passages connecting shadowy, undecorated, stone flagged rooms he knew that he was moving through a landscape that had survived almost unchanged for more than half a millennium. He knew this for a fact because the layout of the rooms and corridors was exactly the same as that which had been inscribed into the tiny plan of the house on the Tudor map he had shown to Appleby only a few days earlier. At the time Smithers had been surprised at Appleby's reaction. After all, the antiquarian had never actually seen the layout of the original Georgian building prior to its demolition. Nor, until today, had he seen the interior of the new house. As a result, he had been unable to link these most recent incarnations with the illustration on the map. Now he knew the truth. Now he knew what Appleby must have realised on Thursday last; why it was he had been so keen to prevent his wife having anything further to do with the plot. There could be no doubt that somehow the house was exercising some infernal influence over Mrs Appleby and her foreman. In all likelihood Mr Appleby himself had now fallen under that same spell.

Smithers stood in the middle of the large, panelled library, filled with heavy wooden shelves and illuminated only by the weak, filtered natural light from the small windows set high up in the stone walls and contemplated the implications of his deductions.

The same house, rebuilt time and time again down the centuries in exactly the same internal form; only the exterior changing with each rebuilding to match the architectural fashion of the time and so provide a modicum of camouflage against overly inquisitive eyes. What the origins of the house were and what purpose it served were mysteries that he doubted would ever be resolved. But it was clear that ancient plot itself had the ability to alter people's perceptions, to guide them in their thoughts and deeds so as to ensure that it continued down the ages in this barely altered form. And that form, the layout of the rooms did at least give some clues as to the guiding principles behind the architecture. As he wandered back through into the main hallway, he pondered the similarity between parts of the building and a monastic establishment. From the sunken chapel on the eastern side of the house to the refectory-like dining hall, he could almost imagine monks moving through the corridors performing their menial tasks.

He climbed the stairs to the first floor and was awed by the sun-dappled space, broken only by the columns that grew out of the floor like beech trees. In his mind's eye he pictured the shrouded monks taking their constitutionals around the cloisters.

He continued further up and further in, climbing to the second storey and losing himself once again in amaze of dark narrow passages lined with tiny, cell-like rooms. Each one contained the memory of a cleric at prayer, their lips mumbling catechisms whilst their joints growing arthritic from long hours knelt on cold stone flags.

Eventually he found what he was looking for – the steep, narrow stairs that led to the flat-topped roof. He clambered up and emerged into the small courtyard, hidden from view by the tiled ridges that rose on all sides and filled, almost entirely, by the strange, organic, wrought iron and glass observatory containing at its heart the huge pintle mounted, dark smoked mirror. He approached the open door to the observatory. The door was a swinging gently back and forth in the damp wind, making the slightest of squeaking noises which, in the absence of any other sounds, not even the singing of birds or the creak of tree branches, was almost reassuring.

Showing more courage and self-control than he would ever have believed possible, he stepped, oh so very carefully, over the thin iron doorstep, and into the room.

He had expected that, in spite of the autumnal chill without, there would be some warmth inside what was in effect a great big glass house. So he was shocked to find that as he stepped inside, his breath billowed out from his lips and his uncovered hands and face felt the sharp nip of an atmosphere far below freezing point. Each breath he took scored his throat and, before he could proceed any further, he was forced to drag his scarf up across his mouth to allow him to breathe without being wracked by violent coughing fits brought on by the icy air crystallizing inside his lungs. He knew instinctively that this was no natural phenomena and was already considering retreating from the freezing glass house into the relative warmth of the autumn air when he heard a new sound.

Once again this was a squeaking, creaking moan, like someone was opening a very old, stiff, heavy door. But this time the sound came not from the door through which he had just stepped, but rather, from the pintle mounting that supported the shadowed mirror in the centre of the room. He stopped in shock and watched as the mirror slowly pivoted round from a near vertical position until it was almost completely flat. He waited, convincing himself that if that was the only movement the mirror made then he could reasonably explain it as the result of wind, gravity or some other natural vibration which caused the mirror to rotate under its own weight to the horizontal.

He must have waited a full minute, not moving, hardly daring to breath, in spite of the cold seeping through to his bones. Then, when there had been no further movement and he had just about convinced himself that this was indeed a natural phenomenon and nothing to cause him further concern, he edged forward to peer carefully over the edge and stare down into the face of the mirror.

He sucked in a breath of icy air in astonishment. The image that filled the mirror was not the expected reflection of himself nor of anything else in that strange iron and glass room. The mirror was filled with movement, shadowy forms and swirling grey mists. At first it was like looking down into a maelstrom of dark thunder clouds or violent black water. He instinctively rocked back from the mirror as he was overwhelmed by a sudden acute attack of vertigo. He stood there for a moment with his eyes tight closed, swaying back and forth and trying desperately to regain his equilibrium. When his mind had stopped trying to make him collapse in a heap on the floor he carefully reopened his eyes and, forewarned now as to what to expect, leant forward again to peer into the mirror.

Once again he was confronted by the swirling mass of fluid grey mist, darkening to an olive black as it swept round the mirror in every tightening circles, like a whirlpool that threatened to suck him down. For a moment he was tempted to put his hand down onto the surface of the mirror – just to check if it was really there – but once again he recognised, at the very edge of his perception, the presence of another influence, something trying to bend his mind to its will. And in that recognition came salvation. The knowledge that pressure was being brought to bear on his mind was enough to break the hold, and the influence dissipated like mist under the morning sun. He jerked his hand back from the surface of the mirror and, as he did so, the mists cleared for but a second and he saw, in the very centre of the vision, a strange eddying pattern of red and orange, a rainbow extension of the dark whirlpool that quickly closed in once again to hide those few, brief flashes of lurid colour.

Smithers backed away, retreating further this time and only stopping when he had almost reached the door. But he never took his eyes off the mirror until he felt his heel tap against the metal doorstep. Then, just as he had shifted his focus and was about to turn to leave this unnaturally cold rooftop folly, he heard the sound again. The creak of metal turning slowly, lazily. He looked back at the centre of the room and saw, to his horror, that it was not the mirror pivoting in its cradle that had caused the noise, but the whole mounting which was slowly twisting, turning to face the door. He stumbled backwards, tripping over the wrought iron step and collapsing into the courtyard which, after the unnatural chill of the mirror room, seemed as warm as a June afternoon. He pulled himself up quickly and edged back to the top of the narrow stairs which led back down into the heart of the house.

He had had enough. His exploration of the house had revealed no hard evidence to support his belief that things were seriously, dangerously wrong and yet, what he had seen and felt had convinced him that there was an unnatural and malignant force at work within these walls. He knew what had to be done and he was now more determined than ever that he should be the one to bring this long, evil chapter of history to an end. Such had been his determination when he set out that morning and, to that end, he had left two, large jerry cans of petrol in the bushes by the gates to the property.

Who can say whether or not poor Smithers truly believed that couple of cans of petrol would be sufficient to start a conflagration that would succeed where so many others down through the centuries had clearly failed. Certainly, as he wove his way back down through the maze of passages at the top of the house and scattered the motes of dust that danced in the beams of sunlight on the first floor, he was convinced in himself that he had to try. By the time he reached the bottom of the stairs and was heading for the front door, any lingering fear had disappeared and he was left with a single resolute thought. The house must burn. It must be destroyed once and for all.

It was a matter of only a few moments to reach the end of the drive, retrieve the jerry cans and a pile of brands, made of bundles of long twigs and kindling bound together with twine, their heads wrapped in torn clothes dipped in petrol. He returned to the house and set about emptying the two large jerry cans of petrol throughout the hall and onto the stairs. In a few minutes, sweating and slightly beside himself as the overpowering stench of the petrol fumes left him light headed, he was stood close to the front door, the cans abandoned at the bottom of the stairs and a lit torch blazing in his grip.

It was then that he heard the cry. A low, pleading moan coming from beyond the closed double doors that led off from the left side of the hallway. He hesitated and listened, wondering if this was just another of the house's attempts to trick him. There it was again. A man's voice, pained, begging, clearly in need of help.

Smithers hesitated only a moment longer, torn as to what to do with his lit torch. The whole hall floor was now awash with petrol and he feared that any moment the fumes might reach up and ignite themselves on the flaming brand. But there was nowhere to put the torch out, and so he was forced to carry it with him as he advanced on the doors and flung them open.

The room into which he advanced was the refectory-like dining chamber. Still bereft of furniture, its corners deep in shadow as the weak sunlight filtered in through the tiny high set windows. The only feature of note was the ornate tiled floor.
The decoration consisted of a pattern of brightly hand painted tiles of scarlet reds, sunflower yellows and shining emerald greens set into the floor of the room, in a design which resembled nothing so much as a whirlpool like that he had seen carved in grey mist in the mirror on the roof of the house. Ingeniously laid with the

length of the tiles steadily diminishing from the outer rim to the innermost eye of the vortex, the illusion was so convincing that the floor, although absolutely flat, appeared to drop away from the walls into the centre of the room. As he stood on the threshold of the room Smithers once again suffered a momentary, intense bout of vertigo as his mind grapple with the idea that he was standing right on the edge of a great pit. He closed his eyes to help ease the effect of the illusion and steadied himself against the wall. Then, hearing the whimpering repeated from the shadows on the far side of the room, he opened his eyes again and, fixing his gaze upon one of the tiny windows high up on the opposite wall, as a means of avoiding looking at the disturbing pattern of the floor, he advanced towards the source of the cries.

As he reached half way across the room he lowered his gaze and saw, moving out of the shadows the familiar figure of Paul Appleby. His face bore a strange, fixed half-smile and he said nothing as he stopped at the very edge of the spiral tiling and waited for Smithers to advance to meet him. The Antiquarian hesitated, suddenly uneasy, not least of all because he had been caught red-handed, about to commit an act of arson upon this man's property.

"Er, Appleby old chap. Are you alright? It's just I heard... well, I heard someone crying out for help."

Appleby said nothing. He just stood at the edge of the shadows and stared out at Smithers with the slightly inane grin painted across his face. The antiquarian noticed a thin trail of drool running down the side of his jaw and hanging from the end of his chin. Although standing upright, Appleby was clearly senseless.

It was then that Smithers heard splashing footsteps in the hall and turned to see Diana Appleby and her old works foreman, Brigham, entering the room through the large double doors. Both were dishevelled and bore the same fixed, glazed expression, saying not a word, simply regarding the intruder with dull, dead eyes. And whilst they made no move to threaten him, Smithers got the definite impression that they were waiting for something to happen; something he was pretty sure he did not want to be around for. He started to move slowly back across the tiled floor, heading for the door whilst keeping a weather eye on the still-motionless figure of Appleby.

"Mrs Appleby, er, lovely to see you. I hope you will excuse my intrusion, I was, umm, I thought I heard someone… came to investigate."

His stuttering excuses drew forth no reaction and he began to contemplate simply slipping past the inert pair and fleeing the house entirely. But just as he reached the very centre of the swirling floor pattern, he heard a familiar and disturbing sound. It was the creak of metal, of a mirror lazily pivoting on it cradle. And it came from directly overhead.

He stopped, stumbling slightly over his own feet, and glanced up, holding the flaming torch high above his head in an attempt to illuminate the high, shadowy ceiling. But there was no ceiling there. He sucked in his breath as he saw a swirling mass of dark grey cloud, turning and building, flowing and tumbling like a torrent over submerged rocks. It was a perfect copy of the image he had seen in the mirror on the roof. No, more than that, it was the image itself. He was somehow looking up at the mirror from below. Vastly increased in scale, this was the whirlpool he had seen from the other side; but he understood straight away that this was no image. He cursed both the evil power of this place and his own foolishness.

As the bruised grey clouds span in ever tighter circles, Smithers realised that he could not only see them but could now hear and feel them as well. What began as a barely audible background rustling was growing by the second and had now transmuted into low, persistent moan that made his teeth ache and his vision blur. At the same time an icy blast of air flooded down from above, from the centre of the maelstrom and he knew that this was the same unnatural cold as he had experienced in the rooftop observatory. How the two could be connected, given that there were two floors between the mirror and the spot on which he now stood, he could not begin to imagine. But he knew with absolute certainty that this was the source of the strange power of the house. Was it a gate, a portal to another dimension? Was it some ephemeral malign force made incarnate? Whatever it was he knew it was unlikely to be good for his health and now, as the low moan mounted to a roar and ice crystals began to form on his hair and clothes, was probably a good time to be leaving.

The torch was guttering in the face of the sub-zero gale that was hammering down from the storm above and the tiled floor was suddenly treacherous underfoot. And now, glancing down in an attempt to stay on his feet as he slid across the floor towards the door, the last bits of the puzzle slid into place. Smithers realised the significance of the flashes of lurid colour he had seen at the heart of the whirlpool in the mirror. Somehow he had been looking straight down onto this floor. He was stood at the heart of a representation in fired clay of the strange supernatural phenomena that raged above his head.

And now the fear returned. Smithers started to pick up speed and trot towards the door. But the floor itself now seemed to be moving beneath the sheen of ice that coated the tiles. The great circular pattern was starting to rotate, a reflection of the swirling tumult above. Worse still, the whole floor appeared to be tilting so that suddenly he was trying to slither and scramble up a slope... or the tumbling face of a whirlpool. He was close to the edge now, almost within reach of safety, but the floor was turning and tilting too fast. There was no way he would make it before he lost his footing and slipped down into the great maw that had opened up behind him. Still grasping his torch, he threw himself forward to claw at the outer edge of the pattern, at the solid, reliable, steady, un-patterned floor that refused to be a part of this madness. He almost made it. His fingers closed around the very edge of the tiling and he hung on for dear life as the winds howled around him and the moaning growl of the hurricane deafened him. The torch, still bearing a tiny flickering flame, skittered out of his fingers and slid away across the floor, right out of the door and into the hall. The hall that was still awash with petrol.

There was a mighty roar as the petrol fumes ignited and a wall of flame billowed through the door into the chaotic dining room. Diana Appleby, stood just inside the door but still showing no sign of emotion in the face of the tumultuous events, was blown sideways and ended up as a crumpled heap in one darkened, flame-flickered corner of the room.

Brigham was not so fortunate. The force of the blast picked him up and cast him headlong over the prostrate Smithers straight into the ceramic whirlpool. He smashed into the steep far wall of the swirling pit and slid, headlong, down into the depths. Smithers, still clinging on for dear life, saw the expression on the foreman's face as, moments before he was sucked down into the maw, the house released its psychic hold over his mind and he had a few, brief moments of lucidity to realise his desperate situation and his inevitable fate. Perhaps that was the cruellest trick of all, allowing the man to suffer his terrible death in full control of his mind. The scream that he emitted as he finally disappeared from view was piteous but thankfully short-lived.

For Smithers, shutting out all thought of the terrible fate that had befallen the old site foreman, there was still a chance. His grip on the side of the tiling was firm and, in spite of his age and general lack of physical strength, he was still able to start to pull himself up the steep slope towards safety.

It was then that a shadow fell across him, cutting out the harsh red glow of the fire that raged in the hallway and filled the room with smoke that mingled with the unnatural clouds. He looked up in surprise and saw Appleby stood there staring down, his face hidden in darkness but two faint glints of light, like a tiny pair of stars shining in his eyes.

A wave of relief washed over the old antiquarian.
"Appleby, thank heavens. Here man, give me a hand, won't you?" Smithers voice was a harsh growl as he strained every muscle to drag himself up and away from the swirling pit beneath.

For a moment he thought that perhaps Appleby was going to leave him to his fate, but even as the thought edged its way into the fringes of his mind, the younger man reached down and, grasping Smithers by the lapels of his overcoat, lifted him up and out of the pit in one, almost superhuman, hoist.

Smithers' face broke into a wide smile as he felt himself pulled clear of the pit. It was a smile that was reciprocated on the face of his friend; the first sign of emotion he had shown since he had emerged from the shadows.

The smile remained fixed to his face as he held Smithers out at arm's length. He regarded the old man for a moment with dark, cold, inhuman eyes that revealed an intelligence thousands of years older than the frail human body it was temporarily controlling.

Then, without another word, he cast his friend far out into the void, to plummet, screaming, into the mist shrouded, violent depths.

Almost the moment that the antiquarian plunged to his doom, the chaos began to dissipate. The violent rotation of both pit and storm began to ease and the floor started, slowly, to rise again and regain its previous flat, innocuous form. The deafening noise eased as the swirling clouds evaporated back into the shadows of the ceiling, and the ice encrustations melted away as the temperature rose rapidly, helped considerably by the fire that continued to rage in the hallway.

Paul Appleby stood motionless at the edge of the decorated floor; his face returned to its former vacant expression after the brief, unearthly smile that had infected his visage as Smithers was cast to his doom. His wife lay like a broken doll in the corner of the room.

A howling began deep within the subterranean vaults, and the door to the cellars slammed open as a cursed wind swept up, through the kitchen and out into the hallway. With it came the stench of death and decay, of centuries of putrefaction and corruption. It swept through every room in the house, leaving behind its taint in the form of rotting wood, crumbling walls and broken, rusting ironwork. Only the dining room, with its two human occupants, was spared. There would be time enough for that room later.

As the wind retreated back into the umbral depths, it sucked with it the flames, smoke and remaining petrol, leaving the hallway charred but extinguished. As the last tendrils of the corrupting wind slipped back into the cellars, the door slammed shut and, suddenly, the house was silent.

Except for a faint metallic creak as the mirror turned slowly back to its original position.

Appleby turned away from the edge of the former pit, crossed the room and gently picked up his wife. Still oblivious to all that was happening or even to his own actions, he carried her home, laid her onto her bed and called the doctor to report that she had fallen on the stairs and was in need of medical assistance.

The doctor duly arrived, declared that Diana was suffering from nothing more than mild concussion, prescribed a mild sleeping draught and departed into the restless night. Appleby went down to his study, poured himself a large whisky and sat in his favourite chair, contemplating the sound of the wind and rain battering the windows and wondering idly to himself whether his wife ought to find herself an interest or pastime; something to get her out of the house a bit more.

At the southern end of the village, nestled between the church and the river, lies Long Benton's very own haunted house. No one knows who owns the place, which has been empty longer than anyone in the village can remember, and for time immemorial has been a favourite haunt of reckless young lads seeking to impress their girlfriends. The ivy-covered frontage hides most of the architectural features but everyone is sure that, in its time - maybe a few hundred years ago - it must have been a very desirable residence. There have been suggestions from some quarters that it is in a dangerous condition and should be pulled down. For sure it is in a very run-down state and has witnessed its share of tragedies. Only the previous autumn the old antiquarian was found drowned in the river close by the drainage outflow. It is thought he tumbled down the steep bank, whilst exploring the lands as part of some research he was undertaking. But no one knows for sure and it was, after all, just an accident.

On balance, everyone agrees that the old house adds a bit of much needed local colour to the village and there are even rumours that the wife of Mr Appleby, who sits as secretary on the parish council, is planning on petitioning the county for the building to be listed and so preserve it for future generations.

Something that, I am sure, we can all agree would be of benefit to the whole village.

THE ALDWARK TALES

Better Not Known

As with almost all my stories, the main protagonist of this tale is based very loosely upon a good friend of mine; one who, in this case, has made his life's work the help and understanding of those with mental problems. As such, probably more than anyone else in this book, I feel I owe him an apology for my portrayal of both the institution and the character he has inspired. I think I can safely say for once that the actions and attitudes I have portrayed bear no resemblance what so ever to his true nature.

Better Not Known

Less than half a country mile outside the little
minster town of Southwold, on the Aldwark high
road where it bridges the Old Parish Dyke, stands
the Southwold Sanatorium. This is a charitable
institution, run by the municipal council, tasked
with the care and restraint of those unfortunates
whose diminished mental faculties - either through
age, illness, accident or hereditary misfortune - have
left them unable to cope with the wider world and
who pose some degree of risk either to themselves
or others should they be left unsupervised.

These are not the criminally insane. They pose no
immediate danger to the public and have generally
committed no crimes; at least none that would
condemn them to a lifetime of incarceration.
Indeed, it is a credit to the institute and its dedicated
staff that many of the patients are only fleeting
visitors who, after a suitable period of treatment and
reassurance, are able to return to normal life
supported by family, friends and the wider
community. For them this is a place of refuge, of
rest and of recuperation. A place for which to be
thankful, not fearful.

There is however another, much smaller, class of
patients for whom Southwold Sanatorium is far
more than just a safe port in a fleeting storm. For

these unfortunate men and women it is a permanent home, a secure hospital from which there is little chance they will ever be released. Their state of separation from reality is so acute, the damage wrought on their psyche so severe, that no amount of loving care from friends and family can ever hope to fit them for life in the wider world. Still, patients rather than inmates they are, nevertheless, securely housed against possible escape or self-harm. As a result, though few in number, they command the attentions of the majority of the staff and resources of the institution.

Nor is it just the sanatorium staff who are responsible for the wellbeing of these most difficult and vulnerable of patients. Regular visits from external authorities and specialists are designed to ensure there can be no mistreatment of the inmates and that they receive the most up to date care and attention. It was thus, in his capacity as a visiting psychiatrist, that Leonard Barrowman came to Southwold in the early autumn of nineteen fifty-four.

As Barrowman eased his tall, gangly frame out of the battered old Morris 8, he reflected that there were probably few buildings in the shire more suited both architecturally and atmospherically to the task of confining and caring for the mentally infirm. Built as a workhouse in the eighteen-twenties, its huge, three storey, red-brick, Georgian façade overlooked high walled, stone flagged courtyards that had once provided the only chance of fresh air and exercise for the unfortunate souls whom destitution had forced into a regime that, for many, was little better than prison.

The workhouse had been shut down in nineteen thirty-six when two new coal pits had been opened, providing work for hundreds of men and bringing some small measure of prosperity back to the district after the long bitter years of the Depression. But the great Victorian edifice was not to be left empty for long. With only minor modifications – notably removing the bars from most of the windows, and the addition of soft furnishing and the sort of modern facilities which would have been considered an extravagance in a work house – the stark but majestic building was transformed from a fearful place of harsh incarceration into an enlightened house of healing and care.

Still, as he strode up the gravelled path, towards the rotunda entrance that protruded from the front of the building, the psychiatrist couldn't help but be overawed and slightly cowed by the monolithic brick frontage. No amount of modification and refurbishment could detract from the original intent of this slab of a building, which was to instil fear and awe in the minds of those being brought to its doors for the first time.

After only a few moments at the front desk, listening to Mendelssohn being played on some hidden gramophone, the visitor was shown to a large, high ceiling study lined with shelves containing books, files and journals. There was an unlit fire at one end whilst the other was dominated by an ornate leather topped desk set at an angle across one corner of the room. Two large and extremely comfortable chairs were set in front and to either side of the desk and a third, identical to the others, sat behind. This last was occupied by a tall, thin, moustachioed man with a receding hair line and deep permanent bags under his eyes. Wreathed in smoke from a cigarette that lingered at the corner of his mouth, his taut face carried an air of weary resignation.

Rising to greet his guest, he introduced himself with a slight but friendly smile.

"Chapman. I'm the Senior Administrator here, I run the place on a day to day basis and make most of the non-clinical decisions."

The Senior Administrator had a business-like manner and military bearing which extended to his speech. Sentences were clipped, precise and provided just the necessary information. He wore an off the peg blue suit and a regimental tie, and everything about him indicated a former officer still, after all this time, ill at ease with the transition from military to civilian life.

Gesturing to one of the leather chairs for Barrowman, he returned to his own seat behind the desk. A few pleasantries were exchanged, whilst they waited for a cup of tea to be brought in by a white smocked male nurse, and then Barrowman quickly moved on to the business at hand.

"So the patient I have been asked to see, Frazier, I have had a look at the notes that were sent over about him but to be frank they look rather... sparse? I was wondering if you could fill me in on some details. I understand from Frank Jennings that there are some unusual aspects about the case but there didn't really seem to be anything concrete about that in the notes."

"Unusual aspects. Yes, that would be one way of putting it. Jennings is a master of understatement as usual."

The Senior Administrator studied his guest for a moment before continuing.

"The boy has what you might call a 'gift'. Or perhaps that should be a curse given how his life has progressed to date. At least, he believes he has it and that belief seems to be the main factor affecting his state of mind."

"Go on."

Sat far back into his deep leather chair, Chapman sucked greedily on his cigarette, drawing the smoke deep into lungs and holding it there for a moment, eyes half closed, a look of blissful peace etched onto his deeply lined face. After this momentary interlude he continued.

"Frazier came to us in the January of nineteen forty-six at the age of twelve. He had been orphaned in forty-one during the Nottingham blitz and then evacuated out of the city to a farm at Northwold Parva. Spent the rest of the war there. As a result we don't really know much about him before seven years old. As far as we know he had no surviving relatives at the time of his evacuation. There may of course be others still alive but to be honest, in all the chaos at the end of the war and with so many records destroyed, we haven't been able to trace any of them. Between you and me, I get the feeling that any who were still around will probably have covered their tracks pretty well."

Barrowman was getting slightly annoyed at the way Chapman was skirting around the subject, hesitating to make clear what the boy was supposed to be able to do. It was as if he feared that by laying the case out plainly he would open himself up to ridicule.

"Why? I mean I know people can be unsettled by mental illness but what is so special about this man?"

Chapman looked his guest straight in the eye as he replied.

"If he touches you he will tell you how and when you will die. And he is always right."

The pronouncement hung in the air between them for a moment; Chapman waiting to see what response his statement would invoke, whilst Barrowman tried to work out if his host really believed what he had just said or was trying to play some elaborate joke. After a moment he replied.

"Can you repeat that for me?"

"I said, if Frazier touches you, he will be compelled to tell you how and when you will die. He has no control over it and after he has made his prophecy he will have a violent seizure, before entering a prolonged catatonic state. And whatever he says at that moment has, to date, proved to be one hundred percent accurate. As far as we can assess."

The young psychiatrist sat in stunned silence for a moment. Not quite sure what to make of the tale he had just been told. Seeing that he would get no immediate response from his visitor, Chapman continued.

"The man's 'gift' can be unsettling, even to those of us who have come to terms with our fates. Given half the chance I think most people would probably rather just forget about young Frazier and his pronouncements."

Finally Barrowman was compelled to speak.

"You talk as if you believe he really can predict the future?"

Chapman didn't reply to this directly but continued his narrative. Barrowman was slightly surprised by this apparent ill-mannered behaviour but put it aside, assuming that the administrator would come round to answering his question in his own good time.

"You remember Professor Spence from the university hospital?"

Barrowman nodded. "I attended a number of his lectures before the war. I have at least three or four of his works on the shelf in my study at home. I assumed he retired years ago."

"Hmm. Well, Spence was one of the external assessors we used for the more difficult cases. Also provided oversight for our own permanent staff. He happened to be here the day they brought Frazier in, in early forty-six. For some reason he was very interested in the lad, as he was then. Later on, once the boy was in a fit state to talk of course, he did the initial interviews with him. Must have spent several weeks working with him on and off, in between his other work. Seemed quite taken with the boy. Seemed convinced that he could help him, get him well again and have him released into the open wards or even back out into society completely. Seemed to think it was only a matter of time and was continuously giving the most glowing reports on his progress."

Chapman shook his head as he leaned forward, stubbed out the last remains of his cigarette in the overflowing ashtray and immediately reached for the teak wood box on his desk to retrieve and light another.

"No one was paying that much attention to the lad at that point. Only Spence was having any real time with him, getting any sense out of him, and otherwise he hardly said a word to any of the nurses or the rest of the staff and patients. Not unusual for new admissions.

And then one Thursday afternoon, Spence came to my office. I had only been in the post a few months then – I'm an administrator you understand, not a doctor. Came into the job after demob. Used to work for the Corporation before the war. Anyway, I was still finding my feet and deferred to Spence on just about everything to do with the patients. He was the medical man after all."

Another hesitation as he drew on his cigarette and blew the smoke up to the ceiling where it hung, misty blue, in the fading late afternoon sunlight.

"That day he was a changed man. Alternately ranting one minute and muttering murderously under his breath the next. At one point I thought I was going to end up having him as a guest here. It was a remarkable transformation. He'd always been very relaxed, patient, brilliant with the patients and the staff alike. Never raised his voice, never seemed to have a bad word to say about anyone. It was a real shock to see him in such a state."

Chapman stared into space for a moment, clearly recalling the day in his mind's eye.

"He said he was leaving. Chucking it all in. Said he would have nothing more to do with the sanatorium or the university. Said he had done enough, done his duty, and he was retiring with immediate effect. But he had one last instruction, one last clinical assessment to make before he went."

The head of the institute leaned forward in his chair as he continued and picked up the brown file from the desk.

"He was sat right there, where you are now, and he made me get out a piece of headed notepaper, the ones we use for official business and entries in the records. He sat there in front of me and wrote out his last official recommendation. It only took him a few minutes. Then he stood up, shook my hand and left without another word. Never saw him again."

Chapman dropped the file across the desk in front of Barrowman before easing back into his chair.

"Take a look at the file. First paper on top. See what he wrote."

Somewhat hesitantly, Barrowman opened the file and withdrew the single, headed sheet that lay on top. It was written in pen in a tight, tidy, almost copperplate, hand. Only a few, apparently unforced, errors and slips revealed the haste with which it had been completed.

Case No. SS46/023

Final psychiatric assessment of Peter Raymond Frazier, conducted at Southwold Sanatorium 25th March 1946.

Please refer to previous notes for background to this case.

In spite of a series of false dawns as outlined in earlier assessments, Frazier has shown no significant sign of improvement since he was admitted to Southwold Sanatorium on 3rd March. He persists in his fantasies that he has the ability to predict the nature and timing of a person's death through physical contact and, in spite of many hours of discussion and therapy, has refused to be dissuaded from this belief.

Whilst this fantasy per se does not render the patient a danger either to himself or others, each manifestation of the delusion results in a severe deterioration in the patient's state of mind which, in its most extreme manifestations, can result in complete catatonia for several hours or even days.

It was clear to me from the first interview that the key to controlling or even curing Frazier's psychosis rested with the ability to convince him that his predictions were nothing more than a consequence of his mental instability and that any subsequent deaths which might have occurred were purely coincidental.
Unfortunately he has been unwilling to accept this reassurance and as a result I have been unable to make any progress with his treatment.

I have reluctantly come to the conclusion that Frazier's history and personal experience both prior to his admission to Southwold Sanitorium and during his time under our care, precludes any possibility of disabusing him of his notions of supernatural powers and that consequently any future treatment should be directed towards ensuring his long term care and, where possible, comfort as a permanent secure patient.

He is, in short, incurable.

The note ended with Spence's scrawled signature partly obscured by an official Southwold ink stamp.

Barrowman looked up from the folder with an expression of open shock on his face.

"That's outrageous. How can anyone claim that this is a serious diagnosis? You don't just write someone off because they don't respond to the first thing you try. What about drugs, psychotherapy, ECT? What about simply spending a damn sight more time talking to the lad? Have any of these been tried on Frazier? Did Spence even make a start on any real treatment?"

Chapman shook his head slowly.

"No. He had hardly got started with him before he resigned. Look, I know this is all rather strange and it looks like Spence was out of order but there's one other thing you ought to know. I said that I never saw Spence again after that day, Well, that is true, but it doesn't mean I don't know what happened to him or what led him to act the way he did. I've got a pretty good idea of why he threw it all in and of why he decided Frazier should be locked up permanently."

Barrowman, seething from what he had just read, was hardly mollified but was curious to hear what had become of the Professor.
"Go on."

Chapman rose from his chair and moved over to the window, looking out on the fading day and the low steeple of the minster beyond the trees.

"Spence left in March of forty-six. To be honest, we were so busy here that I didn't really give him much thought that spring and summer. Frazier's condition was very poor for a few months. Then it seemed to improve a little. He became more communicative and to be honest he can be quite an endearing chap once you get to know him. By October I was thinking seriously about getting another assessment done to see if he was fit for release. Most of our resident psychiatric staff seemed to think this was a reasonable possibility. They had been following his progress of course and although he can be a rather nervous fellow, if you didn't know his history you would be hard pressed to find any good reason to claim he was a risk of any sort. Either to himself or others. But the important point was that he had had no further episodes. We maintained a strict no contact policy. He understood the reasons for this and was just as happy with it as we were. He is a bright lad and knew what was best for him."

The Administrator turned to face the room and sat back upon the great, white painted, iron radiator that filled the wall below the window.

"But at the end of October he had another episode. No one knows quite how it happened but he somehow brushed hands with one of our nurses, Bob Croft. It was in the middle of the recreation room in front of a dozen or more people. He simply turned to Bob and said, 'You will die in your sleep after a very long and happy life. I am pleased for you.' Then he collapsed with a massive fit and remained in a catatonic state for over two weeks."

"Lucky Bob." remarked Barrowman without a hint of irony.

Chapman seemed not to have heard the interjection.

"So of course, that put paid to any idea of releasing Frazier. There's no way he could survive out in the real world if he was continually having episodes every time he accidently touched someone. Plus the fact I was seriously worried someone would take exception to his outbursts and give him a damn good thrashing. More to the point it brought home to me the fact that we had been fooling ourselves into thinking that he was getting better, and because of that we had taken no real steps to deal with the root cause of the problem. Of course, at the time most of us still thought the prophecies were just part of an elaborate delusion reinforced by a series if unfortunate coincidences.

Then in early November of forty-six, whilst Frazer was still in his catatonic state, I received a letter from Spence. The first anyone had heard of him since the day he left. Just a single line. It said; 'Ask Frazier how I will die'. That was all."
Barrowman considered the story for a moment.

"So Frazier must have touched Spence at some point before he left and told him how he thought he would die. So what did you do? Did you ask him?"

"Well, no, not straight away. As I said he was still not communicating with anyone. But also, I was concerned that asking the lad about Spence, reminding him of his supposed powers might bring on another fit, cause yet another relapse. So although Frazier began to recover shortly after that, I held off for a few weeks before I decided to talk to him."

"But you did ask him in the end?"

Chapman nodded. "Yes."

"Did he tell you?"

Once again Chapman chose not to answer directly but instead asked a question of his own.

"Do you remember that winter of forty-six, forty-seven?"

His guest laughed mirthlessly. "Of course I do. Coldest one this century. I was just demobbed and had gone up to Oxford in October. I was going to finish my degree since I'd had to suspend it for the duration. Nearly died of cold in my rooms at the college. Couldn't get home at Christmas due to the snow. Most miserable Christmas I ever spent, and that includes the ones when I was out East."

"I didn't know they taught psychiatry at Oxford?"

"They didn't. I was reading theology at St Peters. Just had a year to go. I always planned to enter the priesthood. But then when I came down the following year I realised I was more interested in saving the mind than the soul, so I did a Masters at Kings in London. Finished in forty-nine. Anyway, you were saying. The winter of forty-six."

Chapman picked up the thread of his narrative again. "Yes, or rather early forty-seven. You remember that January and February? Everything frozen solid. Whole country ground to a halt. But back in November we had no idea it was going to be that bad. So when Frazier told me what he had said to Spence I thought it was ludicrous."

Barrowman regarded the administrator grimly.

"I think I can see where this is going."

"I'm sure you can. As I said, I was nervous about raising the question with him because of what effect it might have on his state of mind. But the staff seemed to think it probably wouldn't cause an attack as they had openly discussed his prophecies with him before. It seemed that only the act of prediction itself triggered the catatonic state. So I went ahead and asked the question."

"And the answer?"

"He said that the Professor would die in his own bed, at home. That he would freeze to death."

Barrowman stood up from his chair and walked over to the desk.

"Do you mind?" he asked, indicating towards the wooden cigarette box.

"No, no, go ahead. There are matches by the ashtray."

"Thanks." He lit the cigarette, took a deep draw and tilted his head back to exhale the smoke towards the high ceiling.

"I know I am going to regret asking this question and I think I already know the answer. This is one of those moments when everything changes, isn't it? One of those moments that afterwards you wish you had just walked away from."

Chapman said nothing.

"Okay. So I assume that the professor is indeed dead. How did he die?"

"In his own bed. Froze to death. He and his wife. They had a big place down by the river at Fisherton. Not short of a penny either. Very nice place they had there, if a little isolated. The bodies were found in late March. They'd apparently been dead for a month or more. I went and spoke to some of the neighbours after I found out about it. They said the whole previous summer Spence had been building up stocks of wood and coal for his fires and boiler. Said that come the autumn no one wanted to visit the couple because the house was like Burma. He had the heating stoked up so high you couldn't stay more than a few minutes in the place for fear of getting heat stroke."

Barrowman was wandering the room as he listened, looking at the pictures on the wall of the study. He turned back to Chapman with a question.

"So how is it that he died then, if he had all that fuel?"

"Well apparently he carried on burning fuel like that right into the winter and through into the really bad weather in January and February. By the time the snows had settled in for a couple of weeks they were running out of fuel. You remember what it was like. In the towns it was bad enough but at least there were people around to help if you got into real trouble. Out in the sticks it was a lot more difficult. They didn't have a telephone fitted and the nearest neighbour was half a mile away along the river in the village. Just a short hop on a nice summer's evening but it would be suicidal to try and do it through ten foot snow drifts. So it looks as if they decided to try and wait it out and hope the cold snap would pass sooner rather than later. And of course it didn't. The whole thing was unprecedented. No one could have predicted it would be that severe."

Barrowman returned to his chair but didn't sit down. Instead he stood behind it, leaning against the tall leather back.

"No one except Frazier."

"Quite."

Neither man spoke for a few minutes. Both lost in their own thoughts. It was Barrowman who finally broke the silence.

"So I hope you will excuse me but I have to ask. Have you, um, I mean, what, er…"

Chapman gave a momentary grimace, then turned it into a shallow, mirthless smile.

"Have I been touched by the lad? Been told how I'll die? That what you want to know?"

Barrowman blushed apologetically.

"Well, none of my business I know. Sorry. I was just curious."

"Course you were. Only natural." He hesitated for a moment before continuing. "Yes is the answer. Didn't want to. I'd been very careful about avoiding contact. Who wants to know their fate eh? Better not known I always said. Particularly if you can't do anything to avoid it."

"So what happened? Why did you change your mind?"

Chapman's stiffened slightly as he barked out his reply. Clearly, in spite of his generally calm, business-like manner he was troubled by the memory.

"I didn't as it happens. It was an accident. The lad slipped on the stairs and would have fallen had I not grabbed him. Caught his hand just as he was about to go down. It was instinctive, though I like to think that even if I had had time to consider it I would still have done the same. In spite of the cost."

He paused again for a moment.

"Lung cancer. That's what will do for me. I had one of the doctors check me over and do a few x-rays after the lad told me. Turns out it is already in there. Nothing they can do for me. Got a year or two at most. These things help of course, ease the lungs wonderfully," he waved his cigarette so the thin trail of smoke drifted across in front of his face, "though the Doc says he thinks that's half the problem. Says the Krauts were doing experiments before the war which showed that smokes make you ill. But you know the Krauts and their experiments. What they did in the camps. Wouldn't trust the bastards as far as I can throw them."

He turned and stubbed out the cigarette in the ashtray before turning back to face his guest and holding out his hand.

"Anyway, good to have you on the team. I'll arrange with our head nurse, Wetton, to have a room sorted out as your office and consulting room for when you are here. And he will also arrange access for Frazier once you are ready. But just remember. Don't let him touch you. It's not fair on the lad, causes him great distress and makes his condition even worse. And it really isn't fair on you either. Remember what I said. No matter how curious you might get, no matter what the temptation, don't let the lad do his party trick. Once that genie is out of the bottle it can never be put back in. Until it happens, you just don't understand the impact it has upon you. It changes your whole perspective, if you're not careful it can destroy you, just like it did Spence. It's not worth it.

Remember. Better not known."

Wetton, the slight, bespectacled Charge Nurse who escorted Barrowman through the secure wing to his new office, proved an amiable, talkative chap who clearly took the wellbeing and happiness of the patients very seriously. He possessed what appeared to be an encyclopaedic knowledge of both their conditions and, as far as the psychiatrist could ascertain, pretty much their whole life history. Barrowman suspected that the nurse spent many long, patient hours in the company of his charges, teasing out the obscure snippets of information, the better to help him understand and care for them. The nurse was clearly a contact to be nurtured and developed if he were to get the best out of his interviews with Frazier.

His guide left him at the door, scurrying off down the corridor with a promise to return forthwith bearing a cup of tea.

Barrowman regarded his office with an air of quiet professional satisfaction. Although decorated in an uninspiring institutional white, it was clean, light and airy, dominated by a large window with views out over the exercise yard towards Southwold Minster, beyond the trees in the middle distance. The high ceiling, polished wooden floors and sparse furniture helped counter the relatively small size and ensured it did not feel too cluttered. As a room to put a patient at ease during a consultation it was about as good as he was ever likely to find in an establishment like the sanatorium.

He had retrieved his large, brown, battered Gladstone – a souvenir from his postgraduate days - from the main reception and it was from the depths of this bag that he now retrieved his pipe and tobacco. After a cursory check through the drawers of the desk he settled himself into one of the large leather chairs – a match for those in Chapman's office - that stood on either side of the window. He lit his pipe and opened Frazier's file once again, making sure he hadn't missed anything important before his first meeting, at the same time wondering just how seriously he should take all this talk of precognition. Certainly it seemed the staff here bought into it pretty thoroughly and he couldn't deny there were some fairly remarkable coincidences. But he wasn't ready yet to start considering supernatural answers to seemingly inexplicable events until he had made thoroughly sure he had eliminated any more prosaic reasons.

The first thing he had to do was meet the young man and see exactly what he made of him. All the important stuff that he couldn't learn from a brown folder and the gossip of the sanatorium staff. Only then could he start trying to understand what was going on Frazier's head. Meanwhile he was eagerly awaiting the arrival of the cup of tea.

It was later that same morning. The young man who was shown into the room was tall, angular and painfully thin. With his close shaven head and his vacant expression, he almost reminded Barrowman of some of the unfortunate wretches he had seen in the photos from the German concentration camps at the end of the war. As an overly tall man himself who had spent much of his youth struggling – and failing - to match the build and strength of his fellow students, the psychiatrist felt a stab of sympathy for the man who was being gently guided over to slip into the second chair on the far side of the window from where he stood.

It was only as Wetton carefully shut and locked the door behind him and left doctor and patient alone together, that the first hint of a transformation began to slip cautiously across Frazier's face. If he had not been studying his new charge so closely it is doubtful that Barrowman would ever have noticed it. Where, previously, there had been a blank visage, bereft of any emotion, any acknowledgement of his surroundings, there now appeared the first signs of anxiety, perhaps of fear. The darting eyes, the twitch of his fingers, a slight tic that triggered randomly at the corner of his mouth. All these small indications told Barrowman that his patient was on the verge of attempting to flee, though of course in a locked room, within a secure sanatorium, there was nowhere to which he could flee.

Barrowman turned his attention from Frazier for a few moments, deducing that his close observation might exacerbate the young man's anxiety. He relit and drew on his pipe, and took out a pen from his jacket pocket in preparation for noting down some of his first impressions.
It came as some surprise to the psychiatrist when Frazier suddenly addressed him in a clear and apparently confident voice.

"I don't know you, sir. You are new here."

It was not a question but a statement of fact, almost an accusation.

"Indeed, Peter. My name is Barrowman, and I am here to have a chat with you and see if we can't do something about making life a little more..." he hesitated momentarily, searching for the right word, "...comfortable for you?"

Frazier didn't seem to have heard him.

"You are new here. I haven't seen you before. You shouldn't be here. I don't like new people." He rocked back and forth in his chair, glancing about him as if looking for a means of escape.

Seeing the young man becoming ever more agitated, Barrowman stood and took a step forward, half stretching out as if to place a calming hand on the man's shoulder. The effect was violently instantaneous.

"DON'T TOUCH ME!!!"

Frazier screamed and recoiled back over the arm of the chair, scuttling away into the corner of the room close to the door. Barrowman was so shocked by the reaction that he slumped back into his chair, but with his hand still held out in front of him as if he had forgotten it was there.

The key rattled in the lock and Wetton rushed into the room, accompanied by another nurse unknown to the psychiatrist.

Wetton took in the scene at once, raised his hand to his colleague to halt him at the door, and turned to Frazier.

"It's okay, Pete. Don't worry lad. No one is going to touch you. You're okay. The gentleman just forgot for a moment. He didn't mean no harm. Bob and I will get you back to your room. Okay? You know Bob. You know he is fine. Just like me. You can touch us, it won't hurt. You've done both of us long ago. So let's be getting you out of here, okay?"

Barrowman slowly let his hand drop as he watched the nurse approach his charge and put an arm around his shoulder. He glanced over at the second nurse stood at the door – the man he assumed was the very fortunate Bob Croft about whom he had heard during his meeting with the Administrator. Croft glanced over at the psychiatrist, acknowledging his presence for the first time.

"You okay, sir?"

"Er, yes, yes I'm fine. Stupid of me. I didn't think…"
"It's okay sir, it takes a bit of getting used to at first. A bit of understanding on both sides if you take my meaning. You just have to remember that if he does touch you, the spooky stuff is the least of it – well

for him at least. Poor sod told us it was like sticking your fingers in an electric socket. Terrible pain, then he just spasms and goes into a coma. Can last for days and every time it happens it seems to get worse. Really not sure how much more of this he can take and he lives in permanent fear of new people. Best make sure you are wearing gloves next time you meet him."

Barrowman nodded, still somewhat bemused by how things had gone wrong so quickly.

"Yes I will. Thank you. I... I think it best we leave things for today and I will return tomorrow for another interview. Hopefully under better circumstances."

"Will do, sir."

Croft stepped aside as Wetton led Frazier from the room. The young man seemed to have calmed now and, if anything, had returned to his semi-catatonic state. Neither nurse made any further comment and the door clicked shut behind them, leaving Barrowman alone with his thoughts.

The psychiatrist had taken rooms in the town, in a quiet inn overlooking the grounds of the Minster. He took supper in his room and fortified himself against the events of the day with a number of large brandies. He slept surprisingly soundly, had no dreams he could recollect and awoke, without suffering any apparent ill effects of either the previous day's proceedings or the alcohol, just after dawn.

After a hearty breakfast he proceeded back to the sanatorium, ready to relaunch his investigation into the mind of this disturbing and disturbed young man. Nurse Wetton was not on duty that morning but Croft was there waiting for him in reception, holding pair of surgical gloves which he offered to Barrowman as they walked down the corridor towards the stairs leading to the secure wing of the sanatorium.

Barrowman laughed, "Better than I could come up with," he said, holding up a pair of leather driving gloves. "Not sure even I would be able to understand my scrawl if I had to take my notes wearing these."

Mendelssohn's Italian Symphony echoed through the corridors, ceasing only when they passed through the locked doors at the top of the stairs leading down into the secure wing – or more accurately, the secure basement.

After the relatively light and airy wards and rooms above stairs, descending into the basement of the sanatorium was like stepping back in time to a less enlightened era, when the insane were viewed as criminals to be imprisoned and punished rather than patients to be treated and cured. Whilst it was clear that a great deal of effort had been made to make the place as homely and liveable as possible, in the end there was only so much that whitewash and electric lighting could achieve. The basement was, when all was said and done, a stone vaulted and flagged pit in the ground and no amount of titivation could hide that fact.

The first thing that Barrowman noticed was the almost unnatural silence in the place. In part he ascribed this to the contrast with the floors above where the quiet background music was an ever present, but not unpleasant, accompaniment to daily life. Here there was no such soothing melody to ease the soul and distract from one's daily preoccupations. And yet it was more than just the absence of music that generated such a profound, disturbing silence. It was the lack of any noise at all beyond their footfalls which echoed down the long chamber which ran the whole length of the basement. There were no muffled conversations, no moans, no laughter or crying, no sound at all that could be assigned to the presence of men and women confined behind the doors that lined both sides of the chamber.

Croft seemed to sense Barrowman's unease.

"Every room is sound-proofed," he explained. "Otherwise they all set each other off. It's the same reason we have the secure patients down here. The rooms upstairs can't be sound-proofed and the patients disturb each other terribly. Far better this way so they can get a bit of peace and quiet."

A look of doubt briefly crossed Barrowman's face but he said nothing.

"Here we go sir," Croft continued, stopping in front of one of the metal doors. "Number 7. Mr Frazier."

He pulled a set of keys from his belt and turned the well-oiled lock to open the cell.

"I'll come in with you and make sure Frazier is comfortable and calm with you sir, for both your sakes. Don't want any repeat of last time, do we?"

Barrowman grimaced. "Don't worry, I won't make that mistake again."

The nurse nodded to the white gloves that Barrowman was carrying. "Best put your gloves on then, sir."

And so after the first, rather disastrous, introduction, Barrowman's study of Peter Frazier began in earnest. Every morning, he would arrive at the sanatorium and be taken by one of the nurses to Frazier's cell. There, perched on a stool at the patient's small desk, he would make his notes whilst the patient recounted his childhood, the traumas of the wartime bombings and his subsequent evacuation, and his life since he had arrived at Southwold. It seemed that prior to the blitz of 1941 in which Frazier's family had been killed, he had never shown any signs of any special ability nor psychological disorder.

His 'gift' – if it could be termed as such – had only developed after he had been evacuated to a farm outside of the city. He recalled vividly the first time it manifested, after he had shaken the hand of the farm manager's son – an RAF pilot home on leave to recuperate from some minor injury. He had declared that, contrary to all expectations, the pilot would live to a ripe old age and, like Bob Croft, die in his sleep after a long and happy life. After making this pronouncement Frazier had promptly collapsed and it had been several minutes before he could be revived. A series of further episodes involving various members of the farmer's family and workforce had occurred over the next few months, each followed by a fit and a period of unconsciousness for Frazier. The farmer had even tried to make a bit of money out of his evacuee by charging local villagers to have their fates predicted by the boy.

But things soon took a sour turn when Frazier began to predict the demise of people far sooner than they might have hoped. It came to a head when a local girl, who worked shifts at the Boots factory in the city, was told she would die in an air raid only a week after her visit to the farm. Whilst most people had scoffed at the news and told her not to take it seriously, the girl had decided that, on the particular night in question, she would not take the bus into the city but would instead feign illness and remain at her isolated farm cottage in the Vale. The bombs did indeed fall that night, but not on the factory. Fooled by the elaborate 'Starfish' decoy system of lights and fire set up by the Government to divert air raids away from the cities, the German bombers instead dropped their payload on an almost deserted area of fields and woodland to the south of Nottingham, killing half a dozen cows and just one civilian – a young woman who had apparently been too unwell to travel to work that night and whose cottage had taken a direct hit.

News of Frazier's prediction and its fatal consequences quickly spread through the community. Some said he was cursed, some that he was a witch – such attitudes still lie only just beneath the surface even in the brave new world of post war Britain. In the dark days of the war they were far too easily given credence. More than a few people pointed out that if he had not made his prediction then the woman would have gone to work as usual and would not have lost her life. No one now came voluntarily to have their lifespan determined. Frazier was shunned for the most part, even by the farming family he was living with. And, true to form, those who did not shun him sought him out in order to punish him for his perceived malevolent gift. Beatings became common place and elicited little sympathy from the farmer and his family. They just wanted rid of the boy as soon as possible.

And still the incidents continued. Although no one now came to the farm intentionally to have their future foretold, there were still accidents when a stray hand or an unprotected fist would contact Frazier's skin and draw forth a prediction. As the months turned to years and the war drew to a close, the inexorable passing of time provided more proof of the uncanny accuracy of the boy's prophecies and stirred up yet more fear and resentment. The beatings increased in both frequency and violence and he became more and more reclusive.

What no one but Frazier himself had noticed at this point was that each time he made a prophecy, the reaction became progressively worse. The pain was more intense and the subsequent coma longer. What had initially been just a few minutes became an hour and then several hours. For a long time, no one noticed. Lying alone in the corner of a pig sty or a muddy hollow down by the stream, after having been abandoned by his tormentors, when he awoke the lad would have little idea of how long he had been unconscious and his return to his room at the farmhouse would usually go unremarked.

It wasn't until after the war had ended and life began to return to normal that the question of what to do with the evacuee began to be addressed. Having just turned twelve he was still a minor, still needed schooling, and although he was willing and able to help around the farm, his introverted nature and the fear that he generated in others made him more of a burden than the farmer was now willing to bear. He had no relatives to return to and the Government had far more pressing cases to be concerned about. But in the end it was, inevitably, his affliction that forced the issue.

Frazier did not even remember the details of the events that finally led to him being brought to Southwold. He knew he had touched, or been touched by someone, though whether it was accidental or intentional he had no idea. He knew that as soon as he had made his prophecy, he had collapsed into a coma far deeper and longer than anything the farmer and his wife had seen before. It was enough to panic them into contacting the doctor down in the village. He had examined the boy and arranged to have him taken to hospital from where, after reading his strange history and discussing the matter with the farmer, the doctor had taken the decision to have Frazier transferred to the sanatorium.

Such was the story that Barrowman was able to glean from the young man over dozens of interviews in the late autumn of nineteen fifty-four. Eight years at the sanatorium had added little to the case notes beyond the regular instances of prophecy, fit and subsequent coma. What was clear, reading through the notes was that, as Frazier himself had indicated, each occasion appeared to be worse than the last – at least as far as the length of unconsciousness was concerned. This in itself was worrisome from a purely medical point of view.

Barrowman thought he had at least gained some insight into the nature of the man, there certainly didn't seem to be anything malicious or malevolent about him and he gave every indication of regret when he spoke of those cases where he had given a poor unfortunate soul only a few months to live. The psychiatrist tried to console him with the fact that he had not directly caused the death of anyone, but this seemed to make little difference. As well as being physically frail, there was a slow, but clear and continuing deterioration in Frazier's mental state - something that became more and more apparent as autumn crept towards winter. This was in spite of the fact that there had been no incidents nor resulting fits since Barrowman had arrived at Southwold.

The psychiatrist decided that, should there be no improvement, or at least a stabilising, in Frazier's condition by the close of the year, he would speak to Chapman and arrange for a transfer to a hospital for further assessment and treatment.

As he drove away from the sanatorium in the gathering dusk of the last day of November, there was one other thing that bothered Barrowman. At some point in the last few weeks, he realised, he had stopped doubting the stories about Frazier's prophesying abilities. Having spent so long downplaying the supernatural aspect of the case he, like everyone else at the institution, now simply accepted it as fact, as another symptom of the poor fellow's sickness.

He wondered how it was that he had so quickly strayed from the safe world of science.

The crisis, when it came, was unexpected, sudden and devastating.

It was a miserable day outside the walls of the sanatorium with a winter storm blowing horizontal, freezing rain against the building. The wipers had failed on Barrowman's little car and he had been in a thoroughly foul mood when he arrived at the front desk. Once again the Italian Symphony drifted through the corridors, doing nothing to improve his mood and it was almost a relief to get into the sound-proofed cell where Frazier awaited him.

The young man seemed distracted himself and his distant manner and lack of response to questions, combined with Barrowman's poor humours served to make it a difficult and profoundly unsatisfying session for the psychiatrist. He decided to wrap things up early, put his notebook back into his bag and turned to retrieve his rain-dampened jacket from where it had been slowly drying on the back of the chair. It was only as he turned back towards the bed where Frazier had been sitting that he realised his patient was no longer sat quietly, lost in his own reverie, but was instead, stood right next to him. Before he had time to even realise what was happening, the man had reached out and grasped Barrowman's bare wrist where it was exposed between the top of the glove and his shirt cuff.

"You will die in exactly one year from today, early in the morning. You will be strangled by a man called Albert. It will not be his intention of course but neither will it be an accident. By the time he takes your life you will have lost everything; your reputation, your friends, family, career, everything you held dear. At the last, you will be utterly alone, unloved and unwanted. I am very sorry. It will not be pleasant."

As soon as the last words slipped out of Frazier's mouth, a faint smile creased his lips before his eyes rolled back in his head and he spasmed violently. He released his grip on Barrowman's wrist and slumped sideways. His head slammed into the edge of the table and he collapsed to the ground unconscious.

Barrowman stood frozen for a moment. He could hardly register what had just happened. He had expected that the revelations might have been accompanied by some sensation, cold, heat, electricity... something. But all he felt was the faint warmth on his wrist where Frazier had gripped him for just a few seconds. He shook his head in disbelief and then his old military training kicked in. Seeing his patient slumped on the floor, a livid bruise already beginning to develop on the side of his head, he crouched to check for a pulse. Yes, it was there. Good. Now check to make sure he hasn't swallowed his tongue – no, all good. Then get help. Help. Surely he was beyond that now. One year to live. Strangled. How could that be? Help. He needed to get help.

Barrowman pushed open the door of the cell and ran into the chamber beyond. He saw Wetton stood at the desk at the far end, looking over some notes.

"Wetton! Here quickly man, I need help!"

Without looking to see if the nurse was following he turned back into the cell, to stand over the collapsed form of Peter Frazier; the man who had just pronounced a death sentence upon him.

It was almost two weeks before Barrowman next saw Frazier. The head wound had proved to be superficial, some mild concussion which was of course masked by the deep coma into which the man had slipped after his prophecy. He remained catatonic for ten days but then awoke with no apparent ill effects. Indeed, reports from the sanatorium were that he appeared to be in a better mental state than anyone could remember since he had first been admitted more than eight years previously.

The psychiatrist was, initially at least, unaware of this. He had reported to Chapman immediately after the incident, had briefed him carefully on what had happened – although he had refused to divulge exactly what the details of the prophecy had been. He had then returned to his inn to collect his belongings and driven back down to Oxford through the waning storm. Once back in his lodgings near St Peters, he had opened a bottle of 30 year old Strathisla and had drunk himself to oblivion for the next day and a half.

His resurrection had been slow and painful. The drunken stupor had done nothing to ease his thoughts and the dark shadow of Frazier's pronouncement was still there, waiting, once his mind had cleared sufficiently to comprehend it.

Over the next week his mood swung back and forth from outright denial to mocking disbelief and finally to deep despair. He turned over the statement in his mind again and again, seeking some explanation, some way in which he could logically argue that he could and should disregard the prophecy. He read back through the notes he had made of every interview with Frazier, searching in vain for some indication of trickery, some proof that this was nothing more than a self-serving con man on the make. But in the end he always came back to the same conclusion. Barrowman had no doubt that every word the man had spoken had been the truth. Well, almost every word. There was one lie there, plain to see as if laid out on the table beside them, just waiting to be picked up. He had said he was sorry – 'very sorry' were the words he had used. And yet in that last moment before the fit took him Frazier had been unable to prevent a shadow of a smile drifting across his lips. That had not been a look of sorrow, but rather one of triumph.

Remembering that smile but unable to glean its meaning, Barrowman knew he had only one course of action open to him. He had to return to Southwold and seek the answers he needed from Frazier himself. Finally, as the country, still battered by rolling winter storms, began to prepare for Christmas, Barrowman travelled north again in search of some relief from his purgatory.

The latest storm had slackened by the time Barrowman parked up his car once again outside Southwold Sanatorium. Squally rain whipped around the building and dark clouds scudded across the early afternoon sky, already fading towards an early midwinter sunset. Nurse Wetton was at the reception and he greeted the psychiatrist with a look of great pleasure. There had, it seemed, been much concern amongst the staff – particularly those who had, in times past, shared his experience - for Barrowman's welfare in the wake of his most recent encounter with Frazier. Seeing him back and apparently in good health came as a considerable relief to the Head Nurse. It was, perhaps, because of this, that Wetton did not question Barrowman's request to visit Frazier so late in the day. He chatted to him amiably as he escorted him down to the basement, unlocked the door and then left to continue other duties.

Frazier stood and smiled warmly as Barrowman entered the room, pulling the door closed behind him. It was an unnerving sight. With the exception of the fleeting glimpse of a smile during their last encounter, the psychiatrist had never seen that emotion on the face of his patient. There was no sign of fear, anxiety, or any negative emotion at all. Frazier seemed... happy, delighted almost, to see his visitor.

"Good to see you, Mr Barrowman," he began. "I hope you are feeling better now. I do understand it was a bit of a shock for you at our last meeting."

His voice was clear, strong, confident. There appeared to be no signs of the dissociation that had characterised his previous demeanour. Indeed his manner appeared almost taunting, cocky.

"I am... fine thank you, Frazier. You are looking remarkably well, all things considered."
The young man laughed. Barrowman was stunned. He had actually laughed.
"Oh I think it is considering all things that put me in such a good mood, sir. It has been a very long time since I was able to consider all things like this."

The psychiatrist was both confused and disturbed. This encounter was not proceeding at all as he had expected. He pressed on regardless.

"Do you feel you are making progress then? Is there some sign of a cure to your ailments?"

Frazier chuckled, "Oh progress certainly, but not a cure in the way you might mean sir, no. Let's just say I can see the light at the end of the tunnel. Do take a seat, sir. Don't stand at the door like that. I am sure we have plenty to discuss now. I know you must have a head full of questions for me."

Barrowman moved over to the desk and put down his bag. But he did not remove his jacket, nor did he sit down. He turned to face Frazier once more. The man had not moved from his position, sat on the edge of the bed.

"I need to ask you... I need to know... about what you told me last time I was here. About my..." He faltered as he tried to form the words of his question.

"About your death?" Frazier's smile had somehow transformed into a guilty smirk, like a schoolboy caught pinching sweets at the corner shop.

Barrowman bristled. "I don't know quite what you think is so funny about all of this. It is no laughing matter to be told you are to be murdered in less than a year."

The man's expression changed subtly, becoming perhaps a touch more serious.

"Who said anything about being murdered? I never said that."

"You said I would be strangled. You told me someone would strangle me. What is that if it isn't murder? And why do you sit there as if this is nothing, as if my life and death don't matter?"

"There are many ways in which a man can be strangled, Mr Barrowman, both accidently and intentionally. Besides, in answer to your second point, there are many things worse than death, sir, and I should know. Not just sitting in this cell, not just my life wasted because of this accursed talent that some benighted God on high has seen fit to give me. I have suffered death so many times, one might almost believe I was inured to it."

The psychiatrist was momentarily confused by this change in direction.

"What do you mean?"

"That's the thing, you see. None of you doctors ever bothered to look at the basics, to look at what was really happening with me. You were all so busy trying to pretend that there was some rational, scientific explanation for my predictions, that they were somehow caused by my 'illness', a symptom along with the fits and the comas. You and Spence both. Neither of you took the predictions seriously. Not until they involved you directly of course."

"I don't understand."

"Of course you don't." Frazier was starting to get angry but the underlying amusement remained.

"The visions, predictions, whatever you want to call them, they are not a symptom of my condition, they are the cause. I touch someone. I have an immediate vision of how they are going to die. And then I actually suffer their death. In my mind, I die just as they will. That is my fit. That is what puts me in a coma for days or weeks on end. That is why every time it happens it is worse than the last time!"

He was almost ranting now, rising from the bed, spittle foaming at the corners of his mouth.

"I am twenty years old and I have died hundreds of times! And then I was alive again, just waiting for the next time. Fearing it, knowing that when it comes it will be worse than the last time and there is absolutely nothing I can do to stop it."

He slumped back onto the bed; his breathing calming, his voice returning to its steady, slightly amused tenor.

"Well, now at last I know it will end. I have found a way to make it end. Thanks to you."

He smiled enigmatically.

Now it was Barrowman's turn to raise his voice in anger and frustration. "What do you mean, 'thanks to me'? What does this have to do with me? What are you not telling me?"

"Ah. Now that's the trouble. I can't tell you." The smile widened on Frazier's face, almost as if he was taunting the psychiatrist again.

"Can't or won't?"

Frazier's smile widened into a grin. "Ah, you have me there. A bit of both perhaps."

Barrowman was across the room in a second and had grabbed his young patient by his shirt front, hoisting him from his bed and screaming into his face. Two weeks of frustration and fear boiled over.

"Tell me, you bastard. What do you know? Why will I die in less than a year?"

Frazier struggled but could not pull away from the psychiatrist's grip.
"Oh you'll know soon enough," he scoffed, the leering smile now wide on his face, "but by the time you do work it out it will all be far too late."

The older man released his grip on one of the lapels and drew his fist back into a fist, slamming it into Frazier's sneering visage. The force of the blow threw the younger man back onto the bed. But it didn't wipe the smile from his face. If anything, it was even wider.

"That the best you got, old man? It must really kill you, a man like you who thinks he has such a grasp of things, well educated, fought for your country I suppose, maybe even a bit of a hero in your own mind. And here I am telling you, you are a dead man walking and there is nothing you can do about it. I have you, old man, exactly where I want you. You have already lost everything and you are too stupid to see it."

Barrowman did truly lose it then. He lost everything in a few short moments in that lonely cell beneath the Southwold Sanatorium. Even after nine years, his body had not forgotten how to fight, how to hurt an enemy. But his mind had forgotten, momentarily at least, just how weak Frazier's body truly was. He had forgotten his first sight of the man just a couple of months earlier, how fragile he had seemed, how defenceless.

By the time he remembered it was too late. And then, as he stood over the bloodied, ruined face of his last patient, he finally knew how and why he would die.

"Leonard William Barrowman, you have been found guilty by a jury of your peers of the brutal murder of Peter Frazier. There is no doubt that you committed the act, for you freely admitted as much both at the time of your arrest and again here in this courtroom. Therefore, the only question that needed to be settled was whether or not there were, as you claim, any mitigating circumstances which might absolve you from the charge of murder. With this verdict, that question has now been answered to the satisfaction of this court and I believe you can have no complaint about the decision of the jury. It only remains to decide upon your sentence.

This was a most violent and frenzied attack upon a helpless, sick man who was in no position to defend himself. This court does take careful note the claims of extreme provocation and, having read the testimony of your colleagues concerning the unusual nature of Mr Frazier's illness and his outbursts, we have given much consideration to the assertion that you had been pushed to breaking point and that you lashed out without thought or malicious intent whilst in a state of extreme agitation, having temporarily taken leave of your senses. On the face of it at least this might seem to be a reasonable defence.

However, any such plea for mitigating circumstances, whilst it might be considered reasonable when dealing with a defendant who was a layman with no special training or experience in handling patients with psychiatric disorders, must surely be waived when dealing with a man such as yourself; a trained and qualified expert, who has spent many years treating and caring for the mentally infirm and who, therefore, should be inured against the worst effects of such behaviour, no matter how unpalatable and disturbing it might appear at the time.

Ultimately, you had a choice. You could simply have removed yourself from the root cause of your distress by leaving the patient's room. There was no need for you to remain in his presence when he was in such a disturbed state and one has to ask why it was, therefore, that you chose to stay with the ultimate, some might even say inevitable, consequence of your losing control of yourself and attacking him so brutally and with such vigour and persistence that your colleagues were unable to make a formal identification of the body without recourse to dental records. Such an assault is not the result of a momentary loss of control, however reprehensible that in itself would be. Rather, it indicates to me a determination to inflict real, lasting and serious injury to the victim; to maim or to kill.

In light of these considerations, I can find no reasonable grounds on which to show any leniency with regard to your fate. Under English law there is only one sentence that can be passed upon someone who has committed so heinous a crime as wilful murder.

It is therefore the sentence of this court that you be taken from this place to a lawful prison and thence to a place of execution, there to be hanged by the neck until you are dead.

And may God have mercy upon your soul."

The Daily Bugle

January 31ˢᵗ 1956

Hangman resigns.

Albert Prothero, Britain's longest serving and best known public executioner has announced his retirement with immediate effect. The hangman has been responsible for hundreds of executions in a career spanning more than 30 years. Amongst those upon whom he has served justice during his illustrious years of public service were notorious serial killers, revolutionaries, child murderers and Nazi war criminals.

Whilst it has not been officially confirmed, it is believed that Mr Prothero's decision to resign is as a result of the unfortunate events surrounding the execution of Lawrence Barrowman last December. It will be remembered that, owing to an error in calculations, Barrowman - executed for the brutal murder of a patient in his care - did not die immediately of a broken neck as intended but instead was strangled in a most distressing manner.

Whilst there can be little sympathy for a convicted murderer, the subsequent inquiry findings made clear that justice, "which must always be swift and efficient and should never involve unnecessary suffering on the part of the condemned man" had not been well served by the actions of Mr Prothero and his assistant Henry Parkin. Indeed the inquiry felt that such events could only undermine public confidence in the system of capital punishment that has served this country so well for so long.

This newspaper can only agree with these sentiments and feels it is right and proper that Mr Prothero should have now chosen to take his well-earned retirement after so many years of otherwise unblemished service.

ABOUT THE AUTHOR

Richard Tyndall is an English consultant geologist and part time archaeologist who has spent the last 30 years working on oil rigs around the world and archaeological sites around Britain. When allowed home, he lives with his family - Liz, Alexandra and Phillip – in an ancient village on the Lincolnshire Edge, not too far from the quiet, historic market town of Newark in Nottinghamshire. It is this town, the surrounding villages, and their occupants, which form the inspiration for the fictional and timeless town of Aldwark around which most of Richard's supernatural stories are set.

Other Authors With Green Cat Books

Lisa J Rivers –

Why I have So Many Cats

Winding Down

Searching (Coming 2018)

Luna Felis –

Life Well Lived

Gabriel Eziorobo –

Words Of My Mouth

The Brain Behind Freelance Writing

Mike Herring –

Nature Boy

Glyn Roberts & David Smith –

Prince Porrig And The Calamitous Carbuncle

Peach Berry –

A Bag Of Souls

Michelle DuVal -

The Coach

Sean Gaughan –

And God For His Own

Elijah Barns –

The Witch and Jet Splinters: Part 1. A Bustle In The Hedgerow

Sean P Gaughan –

And God For His Own

David Rollins –

Haiku From The Asylum

Brian N Sigauke –

The Power Of Collectivity

Bridgette Hamilton –

The Break The Crave System…7 Steps to Effortless Lifelong Weight Loss

Michael Keene –

For The Love Of Tom

ARE YOU A WRITER?

We are looking for writers to send in their manuscripts.

If you would like to submit your work, please send a small sample to

books@green-cat.co

GREEN CAT BOOKS

www.green-cat.co/books

Made in the USA
Columbia, SC
11 April 2018